STORIES FROM THE DEEP

THE CHRONICLES OF NEREZIA - 4

This is a work of fiction. Names, characters, organizations, businesses, places, events and incidents either are the product of the author's imagination or are used fictitiously. Any resemblance to actual persons, living or dead, or actual events is entirely coincidental.

STORIES FROM THE DEEP
Copyright © 2025 Claudie Arseneault.

Published by The Kraken Collective
krakencollectivebooks.com

Edited by Dove Cooper.
Cover by Eva I.
Character Portraits by Vanessa Isotton.
Interior Design by Claudie Arseneault.

claudiearseneault.com

All rights reserved. This book or any portion thereof may not be reproduced or used in any manner whatsoever without the express written permission of the publisher except for the use of brief quotations in a book review.

ISBN: 978-1-7389259-6-4

The Chronicles of Nerezia

Awakenings

Flooded Secrets

The Sea Spirit Festival

Stories From the Deep

Motes of Inspiration
(Coming 2025)

Ruined History
(Coming 2025)

Lost Traditions
(Coming 2026)

Tangled Past
(Coming 2026)

Undying Loyalty
(Coming 2026)

THE CHRONICLES OF NEREZIA - 4

Claudie Arseneault

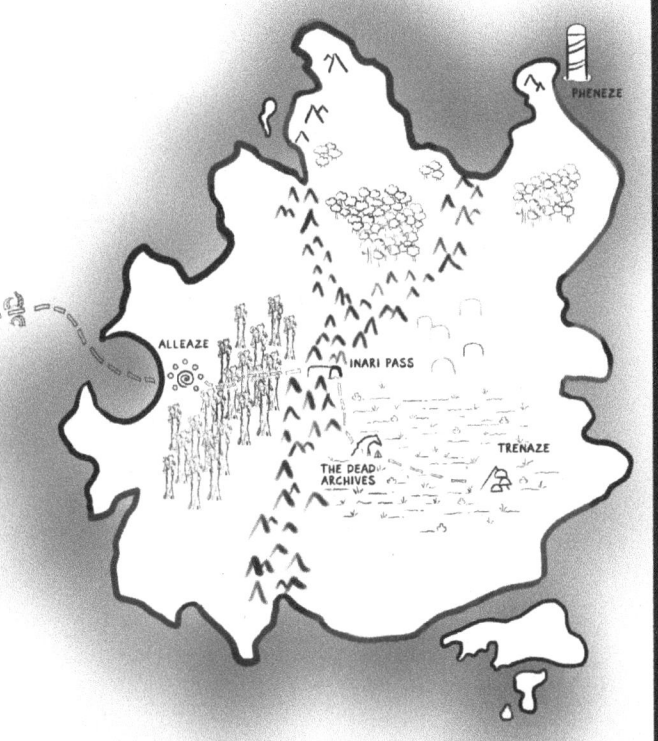

Horace (e/em), Embo Extraordinaire

Excitable and talkative, Horace has taken half-formed skills from eir many failed apprenticeships to become the Wagon's main cook.

Aliyah (they/them), Mysterious Stranger

Left with the strange ability to transform into an eldritch tree and the memory of a mystical forest, the quiet and perceptive Aliyah is on a quest for answers.

Rumi (he/him), Anxious Artificer

Rumi travels the world in a magical Wagon and springs his marvelous creations on the isolated cities of Nerezia. He disguises protectiveness and anxiety under pessimism and grumpiness.

Keza Nesmit (she/her), Thorny Protector

Confident and abrasive, Keza is a thorny companion who knows her worth. Under the spikes hides fierce and loyal love.

So far in
The Chronicles of Nerezia

Horace's trial day as a guard for eir home city of Trenaze should have been simple: stand watch, guide locals to the correct stalls, and guard the giant glyph that maintains one of the city's protective dome—the only thing that keeps away Fragments, shards that haunt the world and possess people.

But when a mysterious figure in a porcelain mask deactivates the dome, Fragments rush into the market, fusing into a monstrous amalgam. They are saved by a strange elf who can transform into a tree-like being, and who dissipated the Fragments with a single, eerie sentence: your story is my story.

When the elf collapses in the middle of the market, Horace carries them to safety, to recover away from the panicked crowd and inevitable questions.

This stranger, Aliyah, has but one desire: to leave Trenaze's safe boundaries and find the forest that haunts their dreams. After an afternoon of board games in their quiet, sharp-witted company, Horace is ready to follow. They leave with Rumi, an anxious artificer and travelling salesman, in his Wandering Wagon of Wondrous Wares, a semi-sentient self-propelling wagon which always remains safe from Fragments.

Life on the road is, for the most part, filled with quiet hours cooking and cleaning, playing board games with eir two companions, or listening to Aliyah's stories of magical worlds. But adventures inevitably find them.

The **first**, at the Dead Archives, a secure waypoint where Horace is once more assaulted by the porcelain-masked figure—an Archivist. They call Aliyah "the Hero", capable of awakening Fragments, and berate em for being too weak to protect them. Horace's skills are immediately tested when Fragments possess dead bodies and attack, and the Wagon's crew barely escapes with their lives.

The **second**, as they seek to cross the Tesrima Ridge, and the pass through the mountain range is flooded. With the help of Keza, an abrasive felnexi who hails from a nearby secret village, they unclog the Fragments-blocked waterways leading to the flood—but their attempt almost takes Rumi's life, and in the process of saving him, Keza reveals her village's existence and is exiled for it. With nowhere to call home anymore, she joins the Wagon crew as they travel to the coastal city of Alleaze.

The **third**, when they arrive there in the middle of the Sea Spirit Festival, a sacred weekslong ritual that determines the course of the city's residents for the coming years. Among the many roles it assigns, the Sea Spirit chooses a Storm Catcher, whose sole purpose is to catch a lightning bolt to re-energize it... and die doing so. Unable to book passage across the ocean while the Festival is ongoing, the crew partakes in games and food to pass time—until the Sea Spirit chooses Aliyah as its Storm Catcher.

Aliyah willingly dives into Alleaze's Bay, having sensed that the Sea Spirit is another collection of Fragments. They dissipate it, calling upon their strange powers, and instead pull a lightning rod from the strange sunken ship at the bottom of the bay, holding it up through a tangle of roots and branches. The permanent Storm

Catcher will irremediably change life in Alleaze, but with the Festival now over, the Wagon crew can hop aboard the *Pegasus* and sail onward, towards the western continent.

No one loves tall tales more than sailors. Legendary captains, mythical creatures, supernatural weather... Every day on the fathomless sea, they sharpen their sense of wonder, their ability to spool story threads from the most benign happenstances. But their stories are not neat little tales of morals. They care not for Heroes, for good and evil. And that, for better or worse, has always made them dangerous.

Archivist Neomi

1

Big Blue Expanse

Horace shook the wooden cup, eir big hand blocking the top opening to keep the dice rattling inside from spilling out, and prayed to the glyphs for a seven or an eight. E *needed* to roll either of them, because otherwise e'd have to pretend it had happened, and Horace didn't know how to lie to save eir life—not even a fake, in-game life. Even thinking about doing it now, with the eyes of eir five fellow players set on em … eir cheeks reddened, and e hurriedly stopped jostling the cup to peer inside.

The eight-sided dice showed a three and a four. So e could either make 34 or 43— insufficient to beat the 62 given to em by Millicent, the old lady sailor on eir right. E *had* to lie about eir result and convince Korrin, who was next to play, on eir left. At least it wasn't Aliyah this time. They could always tell—a combo of their uncanny read on people, months spent together in ever-closer friendship, and Horace's own lack of skill with bluffs.

Eir mind sped through the options. E could pretend to have rolled a double, which in games of Kerva was a better score than any combination of two different digits. But that meant raising the difficulty for Korrin, and the tougher Horace made it for him, the more likely he was to call em on eir bluff rather than accept the declared result, which became his new bar to clear. No, best to stick to lower values. Make it seem like e'd barely scraped past the 62.

How long had e been staring at those dice, thinking of eir lie? E needed to hurry, or they'd know, they'd totally know. Pick a number, any number, something in the sixties—

"Sixty-nine!" e blurted out.

Stunned silence fell on the group of gathered sailors. The gap left by their usual banter was filled by the low wooden creak of the *Pegasus* and the waves crashing against its bow, the background music of the sea.

"Horace…" Aliyah said softly, seated across from em in the small circle of players. "Sixty … nine?"

Their collective reaction flustered and confused Horace, but e couldn't doubt emself. E needed to land this bluff! So e extended the cup to Korrin with a proud "Sixty-nine, yeah!"

The circle erupted in laughter, their voices like a flock of birds taking off. Horace basked in the sound even as e scrambled to understand what e'd done to provoke it. Korrin plucked the cup from eir hands.

"I think I'm gonna call that bluff," he declared, grinning from ear to ear.

"Sixty-*nine*," another repeated with great glee. "This is the best game of kerva I've ever had. Sixty-nine!"

And it sank in, finally, what e'd said, why everyone was besides themselves with laughter. Sixty-*nine*, on eight-sided dice.

"Oh." The tiny sound tumbled out of eir lips. E had been so caught up in the balancing act of a non-threatening lie, e'd forgotten about what was even physically possible. "Oh no…"

E covered eir face in eir hands, red and hot all the way to eir ears, and the other players laughed all over again. Eir embarrassment didn't last, washed away by their honest hilarity. It didn't feel like they were mocking *em*, not personally, and soon Horace was giggling with them at the ludicrous bluff. When the second swell of laughter dampened, Millicent leaned forward, a devious smile on her lips.

"I think Korrin should ride that wave and accept, just for the brazenness of it."

"No way!" he protested. "I've only got the one life left, so I'm taking my blessing."

And so the game rolled on, Korrin shaking the wooden cup with its two eight-sided dice, starting a new round with the results within, no matter its value. Horace had just lost eir last life, but e stayed to watch as the cup was passed from one player to the next, the sailors staring into one another's eyes as they tried to distinguish the lucky from the liars.

It came down to a duel between Millicent and Aliyah, and much banter was had about Aliyah once again reaching finals. In the month since the *Pegasus* had left the coastal city of Alleaze, they had carved themself a reputation as a deadly kerva player, their natural ability to bluff complimenting their ruthless inclination. Where Horace would lie only when necessary, and often badly, Aliyah would declare high numbers for the sake of putting on pressure, giving the next player in line as little leeway as they could. It had taken only a few games for the sailors to start randomly rolling who had the misfortune of following Aliyah in the turn order.

Once, late at night over a drink, Millicent had commented about how fitting it was that the Storm Catcher who had defied fate and survived would be so good at kerva. Horace had tried to figure out what, in everything that had happened, ought to make Aliyah good with bluffs, but e couldn't find anything.

As far as Millicent knew, Aliyah had been chosen by the Sea Spirit to rejuvenate it by catching a lightning bolt, and they should've died in the process, as every Storm Catcher had before. But the Sea Spirit had been made of Fragments—a secret they'd not shared with anyone in Alleaze—and instead of letting the dangerous shards possess them, Aliyah had used their strange powers to dissipate them. Then they'd dragged a lightning rod from the wreckage of the sunken airship at the bottom of the bay and literally rooted it in place, their tree transformation bigger and sturdier than Horace had ever witnessed before. All the growth had stayed there, too, instead of resorbing as it usually did.

None of which had anything to do with games, so Horace had to ask what Millicent meant. She returned eir question with one of her own.

"Do you know what a kerva is?"

Horace had grinned. The sailors had taught em that. "It's when you get a 1 and a 2, considered the highest possible score, and everyone else loses their life!"

She'd laughed. "I meant in the real world, friend, but that's true enough too. Kervas are people who don't give extra tokens to the Sea Spirit when it is time to receive their role for the next cycle. Ever. Most of us, we weigh the balance as much as we can and hope the Sea Spirit will take our desires into account. Kervas choose to rely fully on its decision. It's a level of trust and spirituality for the sacred that few in Alleaze dare to have. For Aliyah to have drawn the Storm Catcher with a single token … and do what they did? It is, in a way, every kerva's dream."

It had not been Aliyah's dream, and although they had recovered from the ordeal, the events in Alleaze had left them quieter and more reserved, closer to the person Horace had first met. Only games managed to melt that layer, as they had in eir home city of Trenaze, but even then, their laughter felt rarer, reined in, cautious. E suspected the presence of the crew, all hailing from the city and life Aliyah had irremediably changed, made it hard for them to relax into their true self. When Horace had asked clumsily if e could help, they'd encouraged em to enjoy the ocean and give them time.

So Horace spent most of eir time at sea with the *Pegasus'* crew. Not at first—in the very early days, e'd found the ocean so fascinating, e'd moved to the prow every morning, leaning on the railing to stare at the waves, so silent that eir friends had been concerned with eir well-being. It was all so big and deep! Endless water, the rich blue of it merging with the sky, devouring everything until the very existence of land seemed dubious, at best. No Fragments broke the horizon line, and Horace had grown so used to the presence of the jagged golden shards that their absence felt surreal, as if the ship had sailed into another world altogether. Every evening, Horace had watched the ocean spread out, infinite, studying the waves until the sun fell across the horizon, setting the water on fire.

In time, the sheer existence of it all had dulled

to a background fact, and eir attention had turned to the second mind-boggling wonder of their sea voyage: the ship itself. It never ceased to amaze em that they could float on such a large vessel, slicing through the waves with impunity, and e wanted to know all about it.

When they'd sailed out of Alleaze, Horace had offered eir help, eager to learn alongside the four new members of the crew selected for this life by the Sea Spirit. Trenaze had no clan for seafaring; what would be the use when the only nearby sea was made of sand? The only time anyone needed a boat was to row on the ever-still waters of the Underlake, under the Nazrima Peak. Not a profession worthy of a clan.

Perhaps that was why e had never found eir place at home. What if eir vocation had been out here, on the wide expanse of water? And at first, it had almost seemed like it. E had helped pull ropes and clean the deck, putting eir considerable strength to good use, and e'd taken up more familiar duties in the kitchen, too. The *Pegasus*' crew loved to talk as they toiled and had as many questions for Horace as e had for them, and e'd chatted so much that between long days under the sun and the nonstop talking, Horace was constantly thirsty. Arduous but pleasant work days followed one another, and when Horace joined Aliyah in their shared bed, it was with the delightful feeling of having perfectly slotted emself into a group.

It didn't last.

Soon e was failing more complicated knots, getting distracted mid-maneuver and forgetting the next important phase, or losing emself so thoroughly in one task that all eir additional duties fell to the wayside. Millicent tried to help em, corralling em back when Horace's absentmindedness won out on eir determination, or going over maneuvers step by step again to make them more manageable. The other recruits left em behind regardless, their skills growing at a pace e couldn't hope to match.

Horace had seen this pattern one too many times. In Trenaze, e would be a week or two out of being dismissed. Eir place wasn't at the sea, in

Captain Jameela's crew, any more than it'd been in any of Trenaze's clans. But this wasn't Trenaze, and it didn't matter if e didn't perform as well as others, or learn as fast. E could still help, and e did whenever e could. Eir failure stung, a familiar disappointment, but the bite of it had diminished to a small curl of bitterness at eir own struggles. The pressure of success was gone. Horace had already found where e belonged: in Rumi's Wagon of Wondrous Wares, alongside Aliyah and the others, travelling the world until they reached the grove that plagued Aliyah's dreams and solved the mystery behind their powers. It wasn't a vocation, not in the way Trenaze constructed clans and *belonging*, but it filled em with warmth and purpose all the same.

For all that e loved the rhythm of the Wagon life, the *Pegasus* had its own unique cadence. Out on the deck, e no longer experienced the constant background plinking, scraping, and muttering of Rumi's tinker noises. Not that eir small artificer friend didn't still work all the time. He had provided the *Pegasus* crew with its own cold box, so that they could store fresh food on their return journey. He rarely came out of the Wagon, however, and Horace had quickly learned it wasn't only because he kept himself busy. The Wagon's magic diminished the pitch of the ship, and the moment Rumi stepped out, he got sick. Which would have been awful for anyone, but Rumi was too small to retch over the railing and his unfortunate ventures out had ended with him on his knees, ruining the efforts of whoever had last cleaned deck. Which was often Horace—not that e minded when poor Rumi was in such a state! Sailors had tried to help him with single earplugs and ginger drinks, but nothing quite alleviated the nausea, so he stayed in the Wagon, emerging for fresh air only when the sea was so calm it lay flat, a mirror to the horizon.

At the opposite end of the spectrum, Keza *never* returned to the Wagon. She had found a new home in the ship's rigging, climbing ropes and mast with ease, and sometimes using her claws to sprint up the mast itself. She spent an inordinate amount of time curled up in the crow's nest, basking in the sunlight, keeping to herself. Even Horace's daily training sessions with her had slowed; e'd been busy learning to sail, and she'd enjoyed the complete break from any interactions with other people. The only thing that could drag her down was getting challenged at kerva, though she liked to pretend she'd win more if her luck wasn't so bad. Horace suspected she'd win more if her bluffs weren't so infuriatingly, intimidatingly high, but Keza enjoyed declaring huge numbers whether her dice had given it to her or not. Each to their own.

Eir favourite part of the sea life came long after sundown, when sailors gathered around swinging lanterns, their dim light casting dancing shadows as they all sat in a circle. They passed around bottles of alcohol so strong it burned eir throat and cast their voices in low registers as they exchanged haunting tales of the sea's mysteries.

"More than fish roam the ocean's waters," they would say one night. "Things far more cunning and deadly than the Fragments of the land. Things that sing in eerie pitches, or whisper to you in the night, soft voices promising treasures and adventures, promising warmth and power, promising your heart's desire, if you but swim with them."

Horace couldn't help emself and perked eir ears every night for the strange chants, but only the constant murmur of the sea reached em. Another night, Gauvranne—the ship's only felnexi besides Keza—told them not of dangerous creatures, but of deadly weather.

"Fog so thick and endless it pushed sailors to madness, cut them from the world and drove them to a quick jump overboard, seeking reprieve in the infinite depths."

Somehow, that felt scarier to Horace than the voices, and e found emself thanking the glyphs for the clear and windy days that followed. Not a trace of fog to slip into eir mind, twisting it. But eir favourite tale of all was the one Captain Jameela—the first person Horace had ever met who used more than one pronouns—told. Most evenings, they sat at the edge of the circle, curved pipe clasped between black-painted lips, their stocky dwarven body almost completely in shadows. But after several nights of badgering from the crew, they finally took the centrepiece barrel and shared their own legend.

"Those who sail the ocean are few and far between, and together they form links in a chain that connect disparate cities across Nerezia, their paths intersecting only when chance or fate brings them to the same port at the same time," Jameela had started. "And of all the tips and tales passed down, all the legends of the seas shared from one to another, there is one that always returns, a recursive wave of terror, a beast known from Alleaze to Virze and from Pheneze to Cinnize… as the kraken."

They all hushed, a few sailors exchanging knowing looks or nudging each other with their elbows. Jameela took a long draft of her pipe, exhaled it, and cast her gaze out to the now-dark waves.

"One might think that is all it is: a legend. But I have seen it with my own two eyes, when I was a youngster on my first foray out at sea. A gigantic beast, ten times bigger than the *Pegasus*, naught but an endless shadow, black even under the brightest moon. It swooped under us, devouring the light as easily as it could have devoured us, and we cowered on the deck, praying for the Sea Spirit's protection."

The hushed reverence over the crew was complete, as if the slightest sound could summon the creature itself.

"I do not know why it left us alone. I would dismiss it as a bad dream, but if so, it is one shared by the entire crew. It passed us, shadows trailing long after the main body, and our hearts knew fear until it finally vanished, and the sun seemed brighter than ever. Other sailors, however, were not so blessed."

Jameela stopped there, taking her time to refill her pipe, her terrible words hanging over the gathered crew.

"In Pheneze lives an elderly elf who used to sail the sea—so old we could add up most of our lifetimes and not match his—and he said to me once, nursing a drink at the rundown tavern seafolks frequent, that he had seen the beast, too, and survived its deadly attack. 'Centuries passed, and still it haunts my dreams,' he declared. A giant, with tentacles so tall they blotted out the moon, so long they could wrap around their vessel and crush it. He clung to planks so long and so hard he forgot half the journey, but to this day, the sound of wood snapping sends him into a frenzied fever."

Foolishly, Horace wished to see the colossal tentacles or the boundless shadow beneath. E wanted to *live* the sea's mystique—and with every day that passed, every new turn of the sun on endless waves, that longing grew. The initial excitement from the ocean's vastness and from the ship's intricacies had dimmed to a low burn. Days followed one another, each one melding into the next, forming a blur of blue waves and blue skies, broken only by the one storm, and that ceaseless monotony weighed on em, sandpaper on eir enthusiasm and optimism, scraping it away until nothing but boredom remained.

Standing at the bow, staring at the relentless waves below, the moon shining through a rare cloud, Horace wondered if speaking eir boredom into existence would help it go away. E gripped the railing and cast eir deep voice out.

"I'm *bored*," e told the sea.

The sea answered. "Tired of the sailor's life?"

Horace startled, only to realize Captain Jameela had walked up to em. E hadn't thought anyone was nearby to hear em complain.

"A bit," e admitted, sheepish.

Jameela offered a sympathetic shrug. "It gets to all of us eventually. No change of scenery here to keep you distracted, nothing new but what we make of it. I love that, though. The stillness, the endlessness … makes me feel out of time, existing in my own little world, free from everybody else's."

"You got the crew. You're not free from them, no?"

Jameela spent a lot of time with the others. They helped with the grittier work, shared evening meals, participated in game nights, and sat in to listen to several storytelling gatherings. On most days, they didn't need to give many orders, but e'd seen how they took command during stormy weather, and how everyone snapped to attention. It had reminded em of Matron Dennys' control over the children, easy and soft until an emergency demanded more.

"Why would I want to be?" Jameela asked. "Now *that* would be boring, I tell ya. Alone with all that? Nah, the sea's best shared, and crews make their own rules."

She laughed and dug into her pockets, no doubt looking for the wooden pipe she never had far from hand. She froze mid-movement, however, and sniffed the air. Her gaze latched to the western horizon, lines of concern barring her forehead.

"Weather's turning, and fast."

The low breeze that had accompanied them most of the evening snapped into a gust, tossing Horace's curls about. E stared at where Jameela was looking, hoping to see what had made them say that. For a moment, the horizon didn't seem any different—but then e glimpsed it, darker lines against the night sky.

"Those are clouds? Storm clouds."

"Sure are, and they're gatherin' like they've been called to receive their Guidance. I don't think we can dodge that one."

2

Golden Storm

They did not dodge the storm.

The occasional gusts of wind turned into a constant howl, and the calm sea rose in ever-bigger waves. At Jameela's request, Horace set out to find and warn the entire Wagon crew. E found Keza first—or rather, she leaped down from the crow's nest, to inquire about the gathering storm. Rain began pouring as she landed next to em, its drumming joining the incessant scream of the wind.

"Jameela thinks we have to weather it," Horace said, and she sprang right back up the rigging to help with the maneuvers, her fur sticking to her lithe body.

Finding Rumi was no hardship, but in the few minutes e needed to cross the rolling deck toward the Wagon, the rain had turned into a thick sleet that obscured vision more than a few feet away. Rumi was already storing and securing his tools when Horace stepped inside the Wagon to warn him.

"A storm, really?" he repeated, nervous sarcasm dripping from his tone. "Wouldn't have guessed!"

He scrambled out of the Wagon, defying seasickness to run around it, claws skittering across the wet boards as he activated its runes. A blue glow surrounded the wheels and sank into the wooden planks beneath. When the next wave crashed against the hull, lifting the ship with it, the Wagon remained perfectly still, glued to the deck.

The rest, however, slid about wildly. Crates, ropes, and all manner of miscellaneous items the crew hadn't secured went rolling. Barrels smacked against the railing, a bucket flew overboard something sharp hit the back of Horace's knee in the chaos. E fell forward, chin hitting the deck and making em bite eir tongue. The rough wood scraped against eir arm as e slid and tumbled until e struck the railing and managed to grab it, stopping emself. Eir heart pounded in eir chest, its hammering covering the incessant rain and wind. This was getting dire far quicker than any other storms they'd encountered.

An old, wrinkled hand extended in front of eir face. Millicent, ever watching over em. Horace seized the offered help, and she pulled em up before providing a rope. Her thin, grey hair stuck in her eyes, but she had no trouble keeping her footing.

"Secured it for you. It takes only a pinch of bad luck to get you overboard, and that'd be a real shame."

E thanked her, but rumbling thunder covered eir voice. She nodded anyway and left em to it, vanishing through sleeting rain to keep the ship afloat.

A flash of lightning lit the sky, and in the brief light, Horace spotted Keza climbing the railing, claws out as she sped across ropes and ladders, shouting something about the rigging being stuck. E still needed to find Aliyah, though by now they'd no doubt surmised the dangers on their own.

E pushed through the wind toward the stern, but a high-pitched scream cut short eir search. Terror dripped from it, setting it apart from the working-through-a-storm yelling and bustling. Horace whirled around, half convinced e'd find Aliyah flying overboard, out of reach, even though the voice was nothing like theirs.

E did find them standing by the railing, backlit by … a green-blue gleam? Horace blinked in case it vanished, a trick of eir mind, but no. In the distance, the water was glowing—glowing dark cyan and gold in turn. Or rather, something under the waves did, a large creature of jagged triangles between which the light peeked.

It was swimming straight at them.

"Aliyah!" Horace called.

They didn't turn around or step away. They *leaned forward*, long dark hair whipping in the wind, their tattered cloak snapping about. Horace sprinted across the deck, struggling to keep eir balance as a giant wave hit the *Pegasus*, splashing overboard and threatening to steal eir feet from under em. E grabbed a rope to steady emself, checked eir security was still well affixed, then pushed to Aliyah and clung to the railing besides them, squinting through the rain to see better.

The shifting light sped toward them, and Horace realized that what e had mistaken for a big creature was actually *massive*. It stretched on and on, one thick body of pale glow with a long trail of golden light behind, faster and faster. It had seemed so far—far enough that they could move away from the railing, perhaps even outsail it—and already it was upon them, at least three times the size of the *Pegasus*, its true girth masked by the rough waters. Horace grabbed Aliyah's forearm, eir stomach made of tighter knots than the rigging.

"We have to go," e said.

Go where, to do what, e had no idea. Fear

froze eir mind and body, the sheer immensity of the creature paralyzing em. E hadn't thought anything could give em that vertiginous sense of scale after the endless ocean, yet e had never felt so small, so insignificant.

The beast slowed to a sudden stop under them, and what Horace had mistaken for a trail expanded, eight long appendages spreading out, twisting through the water. The shards once concentrated near the middle edged out in a smooth movement, forming an umbrella around the core, letting more of the swirling gold-and-cyan light shine through as it connected the eight tentacles on which smaller, brighter shards aggregated into circles. Like suckers on a giant cephalopod.

Somewhere deep down, Horace understood that each shard was a Fragment, that a thousand of these travelling together as a single giant squid-like entity could only spell their doom, through wounds and possession alike. But it moved with dazzling colours and unmistakable grace, the light reflecting in thousands of sparkles across the churning water, and for an instant the pure beauty of it filled Horace with joy and e grinned, giddy with excitement at the world's untold wonders.

Three tentacles burst out of the water, spraying Aliyah and em, and terror replaced wonder. The mesmerized crew that had gathered along the railing scattered with screams as one tentacle curled around the mast, wood snapping under its brutal squeeze. Another flung itself across the deck, swiping sideways until it found Korrin. The young elf froze, and his jaw loosened as he stared at the swirling glow leaking from the shards to swirl around his arm. Tiny Fragments clung to him then sunk into his skin, and the tentacle released him. He stumbled forward with a pained gasp, then caught himself. A bright cyan light shone in his eyes as he rushed for the mast, grabbed a rope, and began tying and untying the ropes secured to it, repeating the same maneuver over and over. His lips moved, but Horace couldn't hear the words through the storm.

E turned to Aliyah, their dark figure striking against the shifting hues of the creature. They stared at it, lips parted, eyes wide.

"Aliyah!" e called, hoping to shake them out of the trance. "It's Fragments. Can you...?"

Horace trailed off with a vague gesture. When e had first met Aliyah in Trenaze's Grand Market, they had transformed into an eldritch tree and dissipated a monstrous amalgam of Fragments not unlike this one into mist, pressing their palm against its head and dismissing it with a compelling chant—*your story is my story*. Time and again since, they had run into large gatherings of Fragments, and Aliyah's power had welled up to rise to the challenge.

They had always collapsed, after, but Horace was always there to catch them. And e was now, too, ready to scoop Aliyah up and bring them to safety once this enormous sea creature was gone.

But no inch of Aliyah's skin had morphed to bark yet, and when they turned fearful eyes toward Horace, eir stomach lurched so hard e expected to be sick here and there.

"I can't ... feel anything. I can't feel them."

The storm almost stole their words away, but they pierced through Horace, Aliyah's barely contained panic heightening eir own. How could that be? Aliyah had always sensed Fragments, even through water and rock.

A deep shudder ran through the creature and the sound of a thousand fingernails scraping on metal rolled across the *Pegasus* in an ear-bleeding screech. The tentacle still curled around the mast pulled and snapped it off with a crack louder than any thunder, yanking rigging along as it released it and swung down toward Horace and Aliyah.

Keza came sprinting down the mast as it pitched forward, an orange blur amidst shifting hues of teal and gold, and leaped off as the tentacle dropped it. She used a short rope to swing underneath, momentum carrying her upward and into a somersault. The staff always tied behind her found its way into her grip as she spun midair, and when her curve led her back down, she was perfectly aligned with the tentacle swiping for them.

She swung her staff down, and an arc of pure force scattered rain drops before smashing into the appendage's shards. They dispersed, creating a brief hole in the tentacle through which Keza fell. She landed hard on the deck in front of them as the long arm retracted, the shrieking metal sound intensifying.

The mast smashed into the deck a second after, breaching through the planks and sticking into the hull.

"The ship won't last. Rumi's trying to convince them to hide in the Wagon!" Keza shouted to be heard. "Get your asses in there while I keep this thing at bay."

"Right."

Aliyah's voice contained multitudes—determination and fear, but anger and longing too, bubbling just under the surface. Horace squeezed their hand. They'd have to figure out why they couldn't transform later. For now, they needed reach safety.

"Let's go," e said.

E started toward the Wagon, pulling Aliyah

along as e battled the water and the dangerous pitch of the ship. Behind them, Keza shifted from one foot to another, claws digging into the wood with each step of her balanced dance. Her staff wove in front of her in slow and steady arcs, ready. Horace wanted to stay and fight by her side, to make all eir training worth it, but this was *too much*. E could defend against a savage beast, perhaps a few Fragments, and certainly a human crowd, if need be, but e couldn't tackle giant sea monsters.

Neither could Keza, but Keza had her village's secret technique to keep both Fragments and water at bay, and Keza was grace and balance incarnate. She was a master, and had she lived in Trenaze, she'd be leading a clan, not in exile.

The first tentacle swished for her, sweeping the deck and splashing sea water about. She leaped through the spray, deflecting it with a quick whirl of her staff before bringing the weapon down on the tentacle in a slicing arc before her. This time, the Fragments slammed together, forming a shield, and instead of dispersing them, the forcewave of Keza's attacks bounced off them and rammed back into her. She flew backward, arching with the blow in a way that made it look almost planned, and landed on the deck with a minor splash.

"Horace."

Aliyah yanked their hand out of eirs, bringing em back to their own trials. They'd stopped by the half-broken mast, where Korrin still did and undid his knot ceaselessly, words of prayers on his lips, a pale cyan glow leaking from his eyes.

"Can you help him?" e asked.

Aliyah had torn Horace out of Fragment possession before, at the bottom of Alleaze's bay, but with their powers not responding…

"I have to try," they said.

Defiance rang in their voice, and they stomped through the rain to Korrin, wrapping their thin fingers around his hand and halting his frantic cycle. Rain glistened on their dark skin, catching the light that leaked from Korrin's eyes as he blinked at her, confused. Horace watched for any sign of bark on Aliyah's skin.

"I'm here," they said, their voice entirely devoid of the crackle of power inherent to their tree form.

Korrin snapped to attention regardless. They spun about, releasing the rope to grip Aliyah's shoulder and arm, digging his fingers into them.

"Help ... me..." The words came as a screech of broken glass.

Pleading. A Fragment, pleading to Aliyah, pleading for help. Just like the bodies in the Dead Archives, who'd scratched at Aliyah long after they'd passed out, somehow forcing themselves—

Aliyah gasped, their mouth twisting in pain as Korrin pressed himself closer.

"Vessel ... help..."

Horace rushed between them, grabbing Korrin's shoulder, ready to yank him off Aliyah. They shook their head, a minute movement that stalled em.

"I'm here," they said again. "Come. Your story is *mine*, not his."

Cyan light oozed out Korrin, a hundred

droplets clinging to his skin, sharpening into shards before peeling away, leaving triangular cuts in poor Korrin. Then the droplets slammed into Aliyah. Horace caught them as they staggered back, boots slipping on the slick deck. Eir fingers landed on rough bark. Under them, and along the entire arm, their skin had thickened and changed.

Relief flooded em, but only for an instant. Even as Aliyah regained their footing, Korrin slumped and hit the deck, only to roll along its ever-increasing pitch.

Horace dove after him, splashing through the thin layer of water on deck to grab his wrist and pull him close. Eir own secure rope tugged as e slid, but e managed to scramble back to eir feet, holding the unconscious Korrin still. The incessant rain forced em to blink repeatedly, and the constant effort of keeping balance was taking a heavy toll on eir endurance. Clinging to the mast, Aliyah looked no less exhausted.

"Let's ... move," they said, voice dragging from the fatigue.

Horace scrambled closer and threw the young elf over eir shoulder, offering eir second arm to Aliyah. They arched their eyebrows in surprise.

"I can do both," e said, ignoring eir own tiredness. "Carry him and steady you."

"Carry faster!"

Keza's voice pierced the rumbling storm, across the deck. She leaped into the path of a tentacle snaking toward them—toward Aliyah, no doubt—and knocked it away with a swing from her staff. Another sliced the air at them, and Keza intercepted it then pounced on its writhing body of Fragments as it retracted, to spring upward, jumping high enough to send a shockwave into a third.

This was not a dance she could keep up forever. Or a minute more, most likely. Horace tore eir gaze away, only for it to snag on other crew members with glowing eyes, brought under the Fragments' possession as surely as the colossal creature was dragging their ship under the water. E gripped Korrin and Aliyah tighter. One thing at a time, e admonished eir sinking heart before hurrying across the slippery deck.

In the downpour, only the faint blue glow of runic magic indicated the Wagon's position. It guided them, a beacon in the chaos, its light strangely steady as the ship rocked with each giant wave, its body increasingly sloped as water penetrated its hull where the mast had smashed through. Aliyah clung tight to em, but they weren't looking ahead; they stared backward, at the monstrous soft glow of hundreds of Fragments fused together, menacing cyan and golden light against a blackened sky.

"Nothing's as safe as the Wagon. It can float. Just get in!"

Rumi's high-pitched voice pierced through the pounding rain. His small scaly body was framed by the light of the Wagon; he was standing by the big steps leading inside, the ones nearly as tall as him, glaring up at Jameela. Millicent and other sailors stood behind, untying the lifeboats. The dwarf spread their arms in a wide, uncaring gesture.

"It's still floating," they said, though their

tone held more despair than conviction. "I have crew on it!"

"There's a mast through its deck!" Rumi shrieked.

"As if this thing can't smash your Wagon as easily as the *Pegasus*."

Rumi tilted his chin up. "It won't. They're Fragments, and Fragments leave the Wagon alone. Can you say the same for your rickety lifeboats?"

Before Jameela could form a reply, Keza interrupted. "Everyone inside, *now*!"

She was sprinting across the deck, claws skidding on the drenched planks. Behind her, the kraken reared its tentacles, Fragments glowing in hundreds of triangles. Fear spread through the sailors and they abandoned the lifeboats, rushing for the Wagon's door. Horace followed without waiting to see the kraken swing for them; e barrelled past Rumi and Jameela, lifting Aliyah as e shouldered eir way into the Wagon.

Jameela entered as e was cutting eir security rope, half-stumbling—and Horace had the explanation for their gait as Keza followed, her staff poking at the captain's back. Horace squinted at the pounding rain through the open door, the darkness filling up with a pale golden light but no Rumi. Where was he? Had the monster gotten him? But they hadn't heard a scream, nothing…

Eir heart hammering, Horace let go of eir two charges and squeezed eir head back out. The rain drenched eir hair again, eir curls long flattened by the weight of water. Tentacles hovered above the Wagon, but they didn't smash down, only floated almost inquisitively. Rumi skittered around the wheels, touching runes and levers. Slowly, Horace caught sight of a pouch expanding under their Wagon, *inflating*. Rumi scrambled back in front of it, and his focused frown turned into a grin when he noticed Horace standing there, staring in awe.

"No time for gawking."

As if to prove its point, a great metallic screech filled the air, and the tentacles retracted away from the Wagon. They rose in wide, angry flails, and for a brief moment Horace did exactly what e'd just been told not to: e gawked, taken by the beautiful arcs of light above the ship.

One plunged downward.

"Get inside!" Rumi snapped.

He shoved Horace back with all the strength of his tiny arms, and although Horace let emself be pushed, eir gaze never left the tentacles. It was still locked onto them as the door closed, Rumi slamming it shut just as the massive amalgam of Fragments smashed through the deck, splitting the *Pegasus* in two.

3
Adrift

The Wagon bucked, knocking half its inhabitant off their feet. Horace fell, bum hitting the ground hard, and two more bodies smacked on top of em: Rumi's slick scales, and someone else's. They'd all barely had time to get on their elbows when the Wagon pitched to the side, sending everybody sprawling, a mess of the kitchen's unwashed pots and plates scattering over them—then it righted itself with a dull splash.

For a moment, they stayed still, everyone panting but not daring to move, as if the slightest disturbance might send them flying and spinning again. Rain battered the top of the Wagon, and the muffled metallic screech of the

Fragments pierced the walls, a reminder of the threat outside. When no further jolt followed, Horace slowly pushed emself to eir knees.

E had stirred too soon.

The Wagon leaned strongly on one side, as if lifted from below. It went up and up, everyone sliding with its tilt, then righted itself brutally as something heavy thumped all around them.

Waves. Waves carrying them, all the way up their crest before crashing into them. Water powerful enough to smash a ship to pieces, but the Wagon didn't creak or groan. Didn't even open its cupboards, Horace belatedly noticed. Somehow, they'd all jammed shut for the occasion, the Wagon holding itself tight against the storm.

"It'll hold?" Despite eir effort to contain it, Horace's voice came out as a loud croak.

Rumi pushed up to his feet, his eyes glassy from nausea. Whatever runic wonder had kept the Wagon more stable while on the *Pegasus'* deck had vanished, and he was clearly struggling to hold it together despite the rolling upheavals.

Everyone stared at him—and that everyone was a far tinier number than it should have been. In addition to the unconscious Korrin, who e'd carried inside, and the Captain, who'd entered after Horace, only a handful of crewmates had made it to the Wagon. Nine poor souls, which meant the sixteen missing were…

E squeezed eir eyes, absorbing that information, superposing it with the glimpses of crewfolks under the Fragments' possession, the brief sight of Gauvranne throwing themself overboard, or of other crewmates mindlessly tugging at ropes.

"It'll hold," Rumi said, putting hands on his hips in an attempt to sound confident. For a moment, it looked like he might add more. His tail twitched—once, twice. Then he clacked his teeth and sat on the ground, snout clamped in his fingers, fighting his seasickness.

The crew settled down, squeezing together on the floor while Keza climbed to the rafters. They let the rumbling thunder and pummelling rain fill the silence, quiet as the storm raged outside and sent them listing one way, then another.

The Wagon still didn't groan or creak, didn't make a sound of protest as waves crashed on it and wind battered its door. It floated, on and on in the endless storm, an impromptu and unlikely shelter. Horace couldn't help but think of the long weeks of rain as they travelled down the Tesrima Ridge, the showers ceaselessly tapping the ceiling. The Wagon had felt cramped then, and there'd only been their small party of four. With thirteen … not even the expanded magical interior of the Wagon could make this remotely comfortable.

Still, it was a testament to Rumi's skill with runes that they could even fit, the space inside bigger than the outside. Everything about his Wagon, from its strong inherent personality to the mechanical prowess that allowed wheels to turn into legs and, it seemed, to deploy a floater thick enough to hold them above water, and sturdy enough to survive the storm, proved how far one could go with the right runes. Horace had never seen anyone else pull off such incredible feats with them. E couldn't remember any runes in Alleaze to begin with, and in Trenaze, that knowledge belonged to Clan Maera, and they used it exclusively to uphold the great shield domes protecting the city.

Horace sought Aliyah's gaze. They had curled up in a corner, head against the wall, eyes closed. Judging by the tightness of their lips and the line across their forehead, they weren't relaxing. Horace wanted to crawl closer, but with eir width in these crowded quarters, e'd have to push everyone around. It didn't seem a good idea, even to offer comfort to Aliyah. There was a tension in the air, as if everybody needed something to focus the fear and grief wound tightly in all of them, and e was unwilling to provide an outlet for it.

So they all stayed silent, the rise and fall of the waves the only marker of time, their breaths held fast as they waited for a tentacle to grab them and drag them under.

It never happened.

Hours passed. The sea tossed them about, the all-encompassing waves visible through the

Wagon's lone window. Rare murmurs broke the silence, then Rumi lost his fight against nausea and rushed into his workshop to find a container. It provoked a swell of snorts, half-smiles, and whispers, and while the stench worsened conditions, it lessened some of the underlying tension.

Occasionally, they tilted so hard they caught a glimpse of the sky, dark night clouds slowly dispersing to show a few stars, then lightening entirely. When the sun peeked across the horizon and the waves had become regular, calmer slopes, Rumi clambered up the ladder at the Wagon's centre, pulled a lever, turned a sluggish wheel to release the hatch, then opened it.

Keza slipped past him and out before he could poke his head out. Rumi hissed at her, but waited on the ladder as fresh air wafted into the stale, stinky inside. No one spoke until Keza returned.

"Lots of sea," she said. "Not much else besides."

A shared sigh of relief passed through the crew. No monster pursuing them, ready to crush the Wagon at the first hint of life. But what hope they had didn't last.

"No sign of the *Pegasus*?" Jameela asked.

Keza dropped down to face the Captain. "Not even a piece of wood, no."

Cries of dismay erupted through the surviving crew and several jumped to their feet, alarmed and upset.

"We should've stayed!" one exclaimed.

Another spun toward Rumi. "You trapped us in here."

The sailors responded to the accusation by turning en masse toward the small isixi. They towered over him, and Rumi, eyes still lidded with queasiness, slipped around the ladder as if it could shield him. With emotions running so high, Horace pushed eir way between the crew and eir friend. By eir side, Keza growled a warning.

Jameela raised a hand, snapping a few names to force their attention on her. Tempers cooled as quickly as they'd risen, and she sought Rumi's gaze, hidden as he was behind the ladder and Horace's legs.

"We're on your 'ship' now. Might be a good time to tell us what it can do and how we get out of this crab trap alive, don'tcha think?"

"It floats?" Rumi's voice turned into a high-pitched croak, preemptively reacting to the inevitable wave of horrified anger that washed off the salvaged crew. The small engineer raised both hands in defence. "If it was good at sea, we'd not have waited weeks for the *Pegasus* to leave port!"

"So we'll float aimlessly until we die of hunger or thirst?"

"We have some provisions," Horace interjected, forcing all of eir natural optimism to shine. "And lots of water everywhere, obviously."

Rumi clacked his teeth—annoyance, Horace thought, but e didn't understand what e'd said wrong. When e glanced around, confused, Millicent kindly whispered "Ocean water is no good to drink."

"Look," Rumi said. "The Wagon won't sink, which is more than the *Pegasus* at this time, and

Fragments don't come near it. Not even that awful monster. It seemed like a decent option." He ran his fingers along the ladder. "I know this feels dire, but the Wagon has never failed me before. I trust it. We'll figure something out. I've been brewing ideas for a spinner that could help us out with directions, and I got enough scraps and fabric you lot could build a tiny mast and a sail to hoist up. Water ... water is a priority, I suppose. I'll start there, but I need my space to work."

He meant that. Once he'd sorted out most of the materials for a mast with Jameela and their crew, he dragged the curtains closed over his workshop area, cutting himself off from everyone. Horace stayed nearby while most of the crew heaved the pieces of scrap wood and ropes up, and spilled onto the roof's platform, where fresh air and work could ease their anxiety. E pushed part of the fabric aside once they were gone, peeking to find Rumi sat on the ground, head against his knees. He looked miserable.

"Oh, Rumi."

Rumi's head snapped up and he hissed. "I'd closed that for a reason."

"But you're sick," Horace protested, eir heart sinking. "Can't we help?"

"Sure, go make the waves stop." He plopped his head back down. "I'll be fine. I need silence, and time, and I'll get back to work. No choice."

Horace hated feeling powerless, but wishful thinking wouldn't make the waves stop. Instead, e brought Rumi a glass of water and let eir friend be. At least the crew had all moved outside and, helped by Keza, they were already working on the mast. Keeping their hands and minds busy, no doubt. Only Aliyah had stayed inside, sitting in the very spot they'd occupied for hours. Horace finally slid by their side and squeezed their hand.

"Want to talk about it?" e asked.

E didn't quite know what "it" entailed here, but whatever Aliyah might wish to share, Horace would happily lend an ear.

"Something changed in Alleaze. I do not

understand it yet, but it has impacted my powers. Just as I thought I was beginning to control a fraction of what was transpiring with me…" They raised a hand and stared at their long and frail fingers intently. When nothing happened, they dropped it back with a sigh. "The tree feels distant and my dreams of a grove have receded. Not entirely, but their reoccurrence is far lower."

"Is that … good?" They sounded wistful about it.

"Not when a giant ocean Fragment assaults us and I am unable to stop it."

Their voice cracked, and Horace whirled on them and gripped both of Aliyah's hands. "It's not your fault. You can't be expected to always save everyone!"

Even as the words spilled out of em, Horace remembered the Archivists' obsession with Aliyah. They'd called them the Hero. Twice now, e had run into the mysterious orange-caped people, who all seemed to prefer to offer cryptic riddles rather than help. *They're meant for grand things, I suppose. Saving people, saving worlds—who knows?* That's what Archivist Kol had said. Clearly, he'd been wrong, to some extent.

"I should have been able to," Aliyah retorted. An angry flame burned in their eyes, and they slipped their dark fingers out of eir much bigger, paler hands. "Perhaps it was a mistake to leave the roots around Alleaze's new Storm Catcher. It feels as though I have torn out the part of me that changes in response to the Fragments. But the Fragments are still here. They still come to me. Why else would this creature—"

They stopped, dark eyes boring past Horace as a soft thump landed at the bottom of the ladder. Jameela stared at them, radiating menace despite her short dwarven stature. She swiped her pipe out in a sharp gesture and stuck it between her teeth, keeping it unlit.

"Storm Catcher," she said, and it had lost all trace of the reverence with which others spoke the title. Horace tensed. "Sounds like you've got more than one legend clinging to you. That's the beast of my youth, if a tad more luminous than memory served."

Aliyah pressed their lips together. There was a time when Horace had struggled to read them, but now e knew every tightening of their shoulders, every twitch of their lips, every crinkling of eyes. Their mask was no longer for em, and e knew that under the prideful lift of their chin, they were afraid.

"I did not invite it, and what clings to me does so through no desire of my own."

"Be that as it may." Jameela walked closer, leaning against the wall opposite of them, anger simmering under their pleasant tone. "Look. I belong to the sea. I live in a world of untold dangers and changing weather. I love stories with mystery, where you don't get all the loose ends tied up all neat. But those don't get my ship destroyed and my crew dead, usually. I think we deserve *some* answers. Don'tcha?"

Aliyah's shoulders curled in, and they seemed so terribly small, in their tattered cloak. Their reply was a whisper.

"I do not have the answers you want. I do not know *why* these things happen to me. I know that they do, and I try to make the best of it and hope that this long road of ours will shed light upon it."

Horace knew, or had been told an answer. Guilt tightened eir stomach and closed eir throat as e considered that the Archivists could be right, that Aliyah was some sort of natural Hero with the power to save everyone. But they hadn't saved the *Pegasus* and its sailors—couldn't have saved them. Horace had played with these people, laughed with them, cooked for them, and now they were gone for good, silenced forever.

"But you knew Fragments acted up around you," Jameela continued. "That's what you were saying when I climbed down. The kraken is made of Fragments, and it wanted you."

The underlying accusation broke through Horace's remorse, and e leaned forward, extending a protective arm over Aliyah. "We'd never heard about any kraken when we came on board, let alone that Fragments at sea did this sort of stuff. This isn't their fault. It's no one's fault, and we're all in this together."

"Are we? Cause it sounds to me like you lot have your own big thing going." Jameela raised a palm to forestall eir protest, and added. "I wouldn't mind, but my crew and me, we're not in this to die for your story. That's a sacrifice Storm Catchers do."

They walked away, and Aliyah leaned against Horace, shoulders slumping as Jameela clambered back out of the Wagon. Horace couldn't help but think Storm Catchers didn't get to decide what happened to them, either; the Sea Spirit chose them. The kraken's appearance didn't have the trappings of a sacred ritual, but it didn't feel all that different in that regard—and both, as far as Horace was concerned, were cruel ways to go.

Uneasiness settled over the survivors as they struggled to find a new routine on the small Wagon, every interaction weighed by the sudden absence of two thirds of the *Pegasus'* crew.

Rumi had spent the first two days in his workshop, hammering and tinkering and muttering, coming out only to relieve his mounting nausea or demand quiet from the irritated crew packed in his Wagon—which, no matter how much more spacious on the inside, had never been meant for thirteen. He eventually emerged early one night, holding a strange little copper pump lined with runes which he hooked at the back of the Wagon, dipping one end into the waves. Several sailors had gathered above, staring with bated breath for the result. The runes lit up upon contact with water, a soft blue glow that scattered its hues across the peaceful waves. After a few minutes of tense silence, a faint gurgle added itself to the symphony of the ocean. Rumi cheered, then propped the top open to peek inside, toothy grin stretched wide. Water pooled at the bottom of his tank.

"Don't we have plenty of that?" Horace asked, utterly confused about the goal of this new little contraption.

"This is good for drinking," Rumi declared. "The pump treats it. Without this baby we'd die from thirst before we'd get through our food supplies." He patted it, a father proud of his child, then yawned. "It'll barely do for all of us, but it's better than nothing. And now, back to work."

He did not tell them what he intended to focus on, only stretched from tail to fingertips, then vanished in his workshop again.

On their third night crammed into the Wagon, Jameela brought their crew up above, sat them in a circle with a candle each, and lit those one at a time. Horace could hear them share stories of the deceased through the floorboards, laughter and sobs interspersed as the night went on. E popped eir head once, to offer the tiny barrel of ambrew—the only strong alcohol left in the Wagon—and they rewarded em with cheers.

Slow uneasy days trickled by, the surviving

Pegasus crew eating through their leftover rations, tension rising with every new meal, every day closer to them running out of supplies. Among the subsisting crew, three had previous experience as fishermen and soon had makeshift rods and nets out in an attempt to supplement the food. Millicent and Jameela had sat together and determined their position from the stars above—an act so wondrous it felt as strange and foreign to Horace as the gigantic amalgam of Fragments that had destroyed their vessel—and now all pretended that the meagre sail would suffice to guide them across the vastness of the ocean and to longed-for shores. Everyone had their role to play, save for Korrin who was still recovering from the hundreds of tiny cuts the Fragments had inflicted on him upon leaving his body.

Horace had taken over cooking duties, helped by Aliyah. Every new meal only needed to serve a third of the people it used to, and e could not dice vegetables without hearing the echoes of the missing sailors' wonder and excitement at the cold box and the prospect of fresher food at sea.

The forced proximity exacerbated everyone's mood, which swung as fast as the wind during a storm. Horace did eir best to stay cheerful, teaching whoever was willing to play saira or thorny bush, or bringing food with exaggerated enthusiasm. It helped, especially when e volunteered to declare another sixty-nine at kerva.

Slowly but surely, as the reality of their situation sank in and the raw grief of the early loss made way to a duller ache, the tension between the *Pegasus*' crew and their small group relaxed, and the lingering nervous energy turned to productive endeavours. A week turned into two, and everyone acted as though they could, somehow, sail the ocean on Rumi's Wagon and its floater with naught but a makeshift sail and Captain Jameela's experience.

Only Keza had no time for the pretense, but she shut her mouth, perching herself at the top of the mast whenever she wasn't pestering Rumi about better locomotion—which, he insisted with great exasperation, he was already working on. Rumi himself avoided everyone and had seemed overwhelmed beyond the usual whenever Horace had dared to peek, but he'd refused any help offered. Horace fretted on the other side of the curtain, unsure when to impose, until Keza promised she'd keep an eye on him, too.

She had been at her customary spot, claws deep in the mast's wood and managing to look balanced and relaxed despite the precarious position, when she suddenly perked up, unfurling and stretching as far as her grip would allow, furred hand above her brow to shield her eyes from the sun. Horace stared at her, waiting, until Aliyah grasped eir forearm.

"Horace, look."

E squinted toward where they gestured — where Keza was staring. The waves had a strange shape in the distance.

"Is the ocean broken?" e asked.

Aliyah snorted, the closest sound to a laugh e had heard from them since this ordeal had started.

"One could say that, I suppose." They squeezed eir arm. "It's land."

4

Fireside Stories

The Wagon's floater scraped the bottom of the beach and Rumi hopped into the shallows to activate the runes alongside its frame. With a blue glow and a soft wheeze, air escaped the pouch, which was pulled back into a secure compartment. The metal arcs of the wheels extended into legs, bounding forward to leave the water in a few bouncing strides. The crew clung to the railing, cries varying between awe and trepidation, until the Wagon settled down, legs clicking back into wheels. If it hadn't been for the dingy mast at the top, Horace could have forgotten it had sailed at all.

After a dazed pause, the crew hurried out of

the Wagon, many climbing down its sides to land into the algae-covered sand. Korrin advanced a few steps, lips parted in wonder, then removed his worn boots, flung them aside, and sprinted off, laughing as his bare feet crunched through sand and small rocks. It broke a spell on the others, who went from a hesitant progress to enthusiastic exploration of the beach.

The island was not a particularly large plot of land, as far as Horace could tell—only slightly bigger than Alleaze's bay had been, although that had been an enormous amount of water in itself. A few palm trees at the edge of the beach turned into a forest proper, stretching onto the ground and climbing up the slope of a rocky outcropping that didn't reach high enough to count as a mountain. When two sailors made to dive through the trees, Jameela ordered them back. The rest of the crew instantly gathered around her.

"We'll settle here until we can devise out a better way to sail," she said—and by the meaningful look toward Rumi, she expected him to solve that particular problem. "Anyone's got relevant experience?"

"I do," Millicent replied. "Had an ocean fishing vessel blown off course once. Nothing like this, but we needed a week for repairs, so we had to figure some basics out."

"You're in charge. Get us sorted."

Millicent obliged. They settled at the edges of the beach, with the Wagon and its amenities within easy reach. An area was outlined to dry out fish, another to build a campfire to cook and gather around, a third for shelters to protect them from inevitable rain, and a final one to dig a proper septic tank, far from any water sources. Before any work could be divided, Keza took off "to scout out the island and make sure it was clear of Fragments." Horace suspected she didn't fancy the rest of the work, but she had a good point, so no one protested. Millicent assigned tasks as best as she could, splitting the crew, which seemed grateful to have something to keep them busy. One by one, the sailors left the organization hub to work until only Horace remained. Horace, and the digging for the septic tank.

E grimaced. Millicent patted eir arm.

"Sorry, friend, but your muscles will come in handy there, and as a desert fellow, I don't expect you've got experience using trees for impromptu construction?"

And so, while others debated what parts of the trees could be employed to build makeshift shelters, e trudged back to the Wagon to find a shovel.

When e climbed inside, e discovered Rumi sprawled on the ground, his arms stretched out across the Wagon's wooden floor, his tail curling up. Eir heart clenched, but the fear washed away as e noticed Rumi's claws tip-tapping a soothing rhythm, and the small engineer whispered.

"It's just us now. Just you and me for a while. No more noisy crew. Maybe in the silence I can hear you right, get some good work done on the propeller."

Horace had the distinct impression e'd walked into something not meant to be seen. It felt intimate and vulnerable in a way their isixi friend rarely allowed. So e coughed, an awkward sound that sent Rumi springing up with a yelp.

"Horace!" he exclaimed, dusting himself off in a hurry, his tail twitching in a wide arc. "I tripped. Short nights and all. Not much coordination left." His small arms flailed about as he chuckled and moved the conversation away, never giving Horace time to comment. "Isn't there plenty of work outside to be done?"

"They want me to dig the septic tank. Can you help?"

That confused Rumi. He had to be very tired.

"Oh, not *me* me. You want a shovel! Yes yes, I have a shovel."

He darted into his workshop, and Horace caught a glimpse of the chaos within as the curtain opened. Although Rumi never could keep surfaces empty, his tools usually stayed organized on the magnetized wall, and there was a sense of flow to his workshop. That had vanished, tools and scraps mixed together in bewildering heaps, bolts and metal bits thrown in boxes with carved wooden parts, all spaced haphazardly around. The pile of what looked like a dozen similar prototypes worried Horace more than anything. E had never known Rumi to have more errors than successful trials.

"Difficult work?" e asked.

Rumi huffed. "It's always difficult work. Just couldn't hear myself think with all these people." He stepped out, shutting the curtain behind him with a snap, and offered Horace a strange shovel, its handle broken. "Here you go."

Horace lifted it, and before e could protest, e discovered the handle wasn't broken but folded, and a simple mechanism allowed it to snap back to a longer, less compact form. Horace expanded it, hefting its weight around as e would a weapon before training with it. Rumi's gaze flicked between em and the door, insistent. The message was clearer than the sea.

"Well, I'll get digging," Horace said. "You make sure you rest, Rumi. We'll need all your brain."

Then e was out, leaving eir tired friend to nab what sleep he could, whether sprawled on the Wagon's floor or in his bed. E'd come back to check on him later. With a bit of space and silence, Rumi might be more amenable to friends forcing him to care for himself—whether that meant rounds of *Proteins*, a good meal, or quiet conversation. Horace was more than happy to provide all three. Anything, really, if it helped eir friend feel better.

Eir concern faded as e dove into the dig, the rhythmic physical work dampening the spinning thoughts of eir brain and settling em down. It took em most of the day to get the hole ready, and when e emerged from it, e found a crackling fire and several long fish cooking over it, their slim shapes wreathed in flames.

The mood over the dinner that night was completely different from the time at sea. Fresh wind blew across the beach as they stuffed themselves, spread around in small clumps rather than crammed in the Wagon's tight interior. Most of the *Pegasus*' remaining crew had gathered near Jameela, who had climbed on a rock and was telling a story, gesticulating wildly with their fish on a stick.

Horace, Keza, Rumi, and Aliyah watched from afar, alone together for the first time since the kraken had sunk the ship. It felt almost normal, a night out of the Wagon after a long day of travel, the stars above blanketing the sky while Rumi and Keza bickered about the proper ways to eat fish. The familiar banter was a balm on Horace's heart after the tense silences of their time at sea—Rumi always isolated, Keza up on the makeshift mast, distant as she soaked in the sun and kept her doubts quiet, Aliyah closed off, overwhelmed by the battering of events at their door and the crew's proximity. This back and forth was better, kinder despite its surface teeth. E flopped down in the sand and stared at the night sky, endlessly fascinating, absorbing the quiet moment.

"I ... would like to tell a story. I think it is crucial, for all three of you."

Tension rippled through Aliyah's every

word, and Horace propped emself up on eir elbow. Their two friends fell silent, and the sand rustled as Aliyah brought their tattered cloak closer to them.

"We're ready," Horace said.

E didn't know ready for what, but it seemed important to Aliyah, so e would listen. A smile flitted to their lips at eir encouragement, and they nodded to em, heartened. Their shoulders straightened, and the warm light of the campfire danced on their brown skin as they launched into it, voice rolling out in a low, entrancing tone.

"There was once a ship named the *Sea Spirit*," they said, "but it was not a ship as we know it. It sailed not the waves, but the winds. Above land and water it ventured, its ovoid body wrapped in a majestic snake figure, teal and purple scales glittering in the sun as it navigated from one sprawling city to the next. Travel was easy, then, frequent. It was a matter of leisure, and aboard hopped those with time and wealth aplenty, who could afford its flights of fancy."

"Nothing fanciful about boats," Rumi

muttered. "All stinking wood and endless rocking. Nowhere for peace."

"Not this one," Aliyah said. "This boat held riches the likes of which we no longer hear. It taunted its passengers with it."

Horace sat up, eir heart hammering. E knew this ship, had seen it fly through a storm when the Fragments had possessed em. It had felt so real, so vibrant, so close to the broken frame at the bottom of the Bay, overtaken by coral and algae. For a few days, e had even dreamed of it, the same way Aliyah dreamed of magical worlds. It had faded now, but e clung to their every word, hoping it was the same ship, the same dreams.

Aliyah leaned forward, their ragged hood falling an inch, casting shadows over their sharp cheeks. When tales became involved, Aliyah turned into a different person, words pouring out of their otherwise discreet self, a gravitas gathering around them, commanding attention. Their voice burned with a low ember that shone in their eyes.

"Imagine, if you will, that the hull is a hall, sweeping wooden arches rising, stretching like wings over crimson rugs. Countless tables are bolted to the floor, thick dark wood carved into patterns of feather or scale, each leg a work of art in and of itself. Everything in the hall is such: beautiful details hewn in seatings and tapestries, in the waiters walking around in sharp and well-fitted uniforms, dark sleeves embroidered with feathered snakes, their shining trays lined with crystal glasses. Overwhelming riches, but those who tread the dark rugs know nothing else; they breathe wealth and power, or so they like to believe. The wealth is their story, one they tell with every extravagant piece of jewelry, every coin they burn in a daring gamble. It's a different time. The world mingles, travels. It's a manicured time, its story tailored, controlled."

The cadence of Aliyah's voice slid into a rhythmic, almost chant-like pattern, and a scratch lurked in its tone. Their gaze unfocused, as lost in the immensity of the nearby sea as Horace was in their tale.

"The *Sea Spirit* is a ship of games, of politics, of showmanship. An elven widower spins a wheel, her deceased wife's fortune hanging in the balance, to be multiplied or disappeared when the staccato of fate stops, perhaps taken as suddenly as her love. Down the hall, ambassadors from three of the Empire's southern regions sit, cards in hand, bluffing through games and trade negotiations alike. While the munonoxi has the largest pile of tokens, the clop of hooves under the table betrays their anxiety; they are only winning one of the two ongoing contests.

"All through the hall, laughter and curses erupt according to the players' fate, but none are as noisy as that of a red-scaled isixi, who bellows louder than her small lungs should allow. She is standing on the table, gesticulating as she demands another card, all decorum gone from her mind. But under the obnoxious boisterousness, her eyes are sharp, her memory even sharper. She knows to count the symbols, knows to bait adversaries into complacency, knows how to play affluent patrons and leave with their wealth, her own pool almost unscathed. She knows, too, that the rest of her crew works more easily while all eyes turn to her.

"Life moves quick and loud on the *Sea Spirit*, and past the hall and the smaller fates at play lies a bigger one, a world-changing one. A fabled vault, which opens only in the darkest storms and grants riches to the worthy. Many have tried their luck; many have paid for the presumption with far worse than gold. The Sea Spirit of legends had no love for boisterous captains; the one sailing the winds shows them no more clemency.

"Or so the story goes, to all but those few in the Captain's confidence—all those who know that under every tale hides another."

Aliyah's voice faded, and the fire in their dark eyes along with it. They eased a slow breath out, shoulders slumping with it, as if all of their energy had gone into the tale. And it was a story Horace knew, though that simple fact alone sent eir mind reeling.

"Did you dream of this?" e asked, fear turning eir voice into a squeak.

Aliyah's eyebrows shot up, concern and curiosity warring in their expression. "I did."

"Me too!" e said. "N-not like that, not in as many details, but…"

Horace had never told them everything that had happened during the swim under the Bay, or that Fragments had possessed em. Aliyah stared at em now, concern winning the previous battle.

"I only dream of these after I come into contact with Fragments," they stated, "and you were underwater before I arrived."

Their tone indicated they'd reached the obvious conclusion. Heat flushed eir cheek, but before Horace could admit to anything, Rumi whirled on em.

"You got possessed and didn't tell us?" he asked. "We thought the *swim* had exhausted you."

"I'm fine. I was fine after Aliyah—" E didn't know what they'd done, or even had any proof it'd been them, freeing em. But they'd been there, and that had seemed reason enough to believe it. "There was so much happening, it didn't seem important."

Silence met eir remark. Horace watched as all three of eir friends exchanged meaningful looks, then Aliyah stated with deliberate clarity "What happens to you is always important."

Horace didn't know what to do with *that*. In Trenaze, eir inability to land an apprenticeship had made em a nobody, and many had taken great pains to underscore that tales of eir struggles were unwelcome. It was different, with the Wagon's group, and while it had grown on em, the depths of the change still caught em by surprise. Everyone here cared, no matter the circumstances.

E cleared eir throat. "So why did I dream of them? I'm not you, Aliyah."

"Perhaps the dreams are less an intrinsic part of me than we had thought, and more a consequence of contact with Fragments. Perhaps I am simply better attuned to it, as I am to

Fragments in general." They paused to consider that, and continued. "I do not believe I dream as others do, of fictive imagery to mirror their days. In my sleep I see full lives, dioramas of vivid emotional moments, stories unfolding one after the other, or gathered together. And it … it changes, when we meet Fragments, when I—"

They lifted their hand, palm out, the same as they always did when they touched Fragments to dissipate and absorb them. *Your story is my story.* Words taking on a new meaning, a more literal one. Not only a chant or metaphor, but a fact.

"I'd flip my shit if I dreamed of stuff like that every night," Keza said, breaking the solemnity of the moment.

"That's because your mind is *small*," Rumi retorted.

Keza's tail mysteriously twitched right into his face. She tapped her forehead with a finger, smirking. "Focused is the term you're looking for, shortscales."

The ease with which they bounced off one

another relieved the tightness in Horace's head as heavy thoughts slowly formed in it.

"The *Sea Spirit*," e said, "the ship, that is, the one we dreamed about—it was there. At the bottom of the Bay. It was real, not a dream."

"Indeed," Aliyah confirmed.

Did that mean the dreams e'd had about it were also real? And if the dreams were, what about the Fragments-induced hallucinations? What about the Fragments themselves? All eir life, Horace had known them as sharp pieces that floated, seeking unwary wanderers to possess, often reenacting a single moment until the host died of exhaustion. But throughout their travels, they'd seen them clump together to try to do more mundane tasks, or possess bodies to *speak*. Eir heart pounding, Horace voiced the only conclusion e could think of, the only way e could explain the behaviour.

"They're people?" e asked. "The Fragments are people?"

"*Were* people, I believe." Aliyah tugged on their tattered cloak, bringing it closer to their body. "I dream of them, of their lives and desires and memories."

"And *I'm* weird for not wanting any of that," Keza said. "Sounds awful."

Aliyah did not reply save for a pensive hum. Horace wanted to agree with Keza. E had held Aliyah through so many nights of tossing and turning, e couldn't deny the toll these dreams took on them. Yet at the same time, e craved more of these strange stories Aliyah collected. The world of their dreams—the one e had seen so briefly—had nothing in common with eir present, and it boggled eir mind. E wished to hear every story, discover everything e could.

"I'd take them, if I could," e said. "Even more so if we could ask questions! Wouldn't you want to learn how the *Sea Spirit* flew, Rumi? You could make your Wagon do the same!"

Rumi's mouth opened, then snapped shut as his eyes widened. Horace could see the possibilities careening around his brain echoed in the bounce of his tail. "A flying wagon," he repeated, in awe.

"At least we'd be off this island."

"Oh, I'll get *you* off this island all right, and spare us all your snark." Rumi's retort was almost mechanical, the bite worn off by his own worry about their current predicament.

"Exile the exile?" Keza asked.

"Of course not!" Horace forced cheer in eir voice and slapped a hand over Rumi's shoulder. "He'll get us all off this island, because he's got a genius's brain and we'll all help find him whatever he needs. There's not a problem Rumi can't solve if we don't give him the time."

Rumi's tiny shoulders straightened under Horace's large palm, then he crossed his arms and clacked his teeth in defiance. "That's right. I'll have the Wagon sailing proper. You lot just hang in there and play some game while I do all the hard work."

"Hey, I dug a very big hole today! That was *hard* work, even for me."

Something in eir protest must have been hilarious, because all three others laughed then, and the creases of worry and exhaustion lifted from em. The familiar concert was an essential reminder than even here, stranded on an island in the middle of the ocean and with a terrifying newfound understanding of the world around em, Horace had dear friends e could call home.

No one mentioned the Fragments again, but their hypothesis never left the back of Horace's mind, an idea so big e struggled to comprehend it, or to know what to do with it. For now, it was enough that Aliyah seemed more relaxed, a weight lifted from their shoulders at having shared their conclusion. They would have ample time to work through the implications while stuck on this island.

5

The Inevitable Draw of Beaches

True to his word, Rumi went right to work the following morning, closing the Wagon off as soon as they'd scrounged together an early breakfast. Building their makeshift and hopefully quite temporary encampment offered plenty to do, regardless. Shelters still needed to be constructed, Keza insisted on exploring the island, and the three sailors with the most fishing experience debated the best bait and spots to provide for their next meal. Korrin had teamed up with Phyllis, one of the sailors most skilled with the ropes, and Posk, a brown-furred munonoxi with previous jobs as a carpenter, and the three of them had taken down the mast to make it sturdier for future sailing.

Everybody kept busy, and although the heavy, grieving silence of their time drifting in the Wagon had given way to occasional chats, laughter had grown rare and subdued, the crew's joy while working a ghost of what it had been on the *Pegasus*. Every sailor who had sunk with the ship left an indelible hole in the conversations, an absent voice that could be felt by all those that remained.

On the third morning, eir sanitary pit dig finished, Horace joined the group building new shelters, using trimmed branches and the trees' gigantic leaves. Some of them sprawled longer than Horace's arms, glistening and green, vegetation the likes of which e'd never seen in the desert. E'd been impressed by the tall forest on Alleaze's side of the Tesrima Ridge, but although those stretched upward to the sky, their trunks so large e couldn't surround em with eir arms, their leaves had been small rows of spiky points common to evergreens. It would never cease to fascinate Horace, how varied plant life was across the world, from the thick and barbed leaves of succulents in the deserts, to the endlessly vertical trees outside Alleaze, and now these wonderful specimens. Horace spent as much time waving the long leaves around, making *woosh* sounds, as e did placing them atop their makeshift constructions to build roofs.

Once, eir wide swoops clipped Millicent and the older sailor stumbled, more out of surprise at the large green thing in her face than any real strength in the blow. Unfortunately for Horace, several crew members saw it and surrounded em with fake outrage, each with their own "weapon", ready to avenge her. Horace tanked the first two leaf slaps, too confused to dodge, but before long eir reflexes kicked in, and e brought eir own leaf up as a shield, parrying with it. The sailors cackled and redoubled their efforts, so Horace put everything e had into the spontaneous make-believe fight, grinning ear to ear.

They were still doing this strange dance when Keza discovered them.

"Training without me?" she asked. "I'm wounded."

E turned toward her voice only to find an odd amber sphere flying at eir face. It, too, caught em off guard, and it smacked into eir nose. Tears blurred eir vision from the sudden pain, but through them e thought e saw the ball hit the ground and *bounce*. Keza caught it up again and grinned.

"Found this in the jungle," she said. "There's a couple more. My guess is that it served as protection for some big bug or another? There's a hole here." She flipped it, showing an opening about a third of its width on one side. "Then I kicked it and …"

She trailed off, holding the ball up and kicking it hard at a tree. It hit the trunk, and instead of smashing into a hundred pieces, it bounced off, flying at a weird angle toward the beach with remarkable speed and … going directly for Jameela's head.

It bonked the captain's skull hard, making them drop the bundle of branches they'd been tying with vines, then bounced back in Horace's direction as Jameela spun about with an indignant cry. The ball rolled to eir feet, stopping a few feet away.

"Horace!" Jameela exclaimed. "What do you think you're doing?"

"That was—"

Horace turned to gesture at Keza, but the only trace of her was a quick rustle through the nearby underbrush. She'd left em to take the fall!

"Yeah, Horace," Millicent said, amusement brimming in her voice. "First you slap an old lady with a leaf, and now you throw balls at someone with their back to you?"

"I didn't. I swear I—"

The crew's laughter buried eir protest, and panic rose through Horace. E'd been blamed for mistakes not eir own before, been cut off before e could explain. What would Jameela think, now? E didn't want to be seen as disruptive, or incapable, or—

Cool fingers touched eir arm, and e turned to find Aliyah by eir side, vines and branches in hand. They mouthed a soft "it's all right", and e breathed in deeply. No one glared at em or whispered angry words. They were laughing, in good spirits, a few of them enjoying their own leaf duel. Millicent slapped eir shoulder with a grin, and the tightness in Horace's lungs unwound. They all needed a solid laugh, and it wasn't truly at eir expense. E bent and picked up the ball.

"If we had a second one of these, we could play Three Plateaus." E turned toward the tree line. No need to see Keza to know she was listening in, so e cast eir voice out. "Wouldn't it be so nice if we had someone who knew what to look for that'd go out and find us more of those strange spheres while we toil on the shelters?"

A quick rustle later, and e knew it was only a matter of time. Ball in hand, e turned to the *Pegasus*'s crew. "Well? How about we get some work done, then I'll teach you one of the fiercest sports from home."

Three Plateaus shone by its simplicity. Three teams of three players faced off in a circular arena that had been divided in equal thirds—each representing one of the three flat plateaus on which Trenaze had been built. Another smaller circle delineated "the mountain", a neutral zone in the middle. To mark a point, a team needed to get the ball to fall on their opponent's third. Any hit outside, however, counted as a negative point. In proper arenas, walls about a meter high enclosed the arena and split the thirds, but Horace had to do with dragging much lower tree trunks in place, and using taller sticks as guides for height. The latter might have been enough, but the game wasn't the same without the ball bouncing off the top of the walls, so the trunks would serve as a chaotic replacement. They'd have to get runners to place any balls that escaped back in the neutral zone, too.

"The last rule," Horace said to the gathered group, "is that each player on a team can only employ one of three parts of their body to touch the ball: one uses their hands and arms, the second their feet and legs, and the third the rest of their body. No grabbing the ball."

"That's it?" A dangerous eagerness floated through Keza's tone. "No other rules?"

Horace raked eir brain. There was a good chance e'd forgotten something. Three Plateaus had less moving pieces and rules than saira, but eir memory had never been eir strong suit. E'd gone over the arena lines, how rounds played, how to score points and player specificity, so…

"Oh!" It came back to em, a flash prompted by memories of Trenaze's most scandalous Three Plateaus game. "No touching the other teams' players."

Keza pouted. "But I can aim the ball at their faces, right?"

"Y-yes." Which would hurt a lot more with these stretchy amber balls than it would have with the softer ones at home. "Don't break someone's nose for a point, Keza!"

She grinned at em, sharp teeth adding a layer of viciousness to the expression. "You're no fun."

"I'd like to be on Keza's team," Korrin piped up, fear lacing the request.

The other sailors laughed, but before long they were arguing over the third position, equally eager to *not* face off with the agile felnexi who'd been climbing all over their rigging. Horace let them, instead scanning the beach for Aliyah. They stood a distance back, but e knew they'd listened to every word of eir explanation.

"Come be my Feet," e said.

Aliyah's gaze flicked to the rest of the crew, ending on Jameela. They had avoided one another since their tense discussion inside the Wagon, but Horace refused to let Aliyah miss out on the fun because of it.

"I'm team leader. I decide who's on mine. And we make a good team, no?"

A hint of a smile, a barely perceptible nod, and Horace knew e'd won this. Aliyah shucked their tattered cloak off, removed their boots, and walked over barefoot in the sand with obvious trepidation.

"Thank you, Horace," they said.

Horace wasn't too certain what had earned em the praise when they seemed reluctant to play, but e glowed with the gratefulness nonetheless. All e wanted was for eir friends to play eir hometown game, to experience the intensity of it. E always felt so much better after a few rounds, like eir worries evaporated with all the energy burned. It was a nice afternoon, the sun warm on eir skin, its heat dampened by the sea breeze—a perfect moment to evacuate all that accumulated tension.

Horace stretched eir shoulders and scanned the gathered group, welcoming one last crewmate. Phyllis was a rail-thin human, but e'd seen how quickly she climbed the rigging and tied knots, so e asked her to be their Hands. E always played best as the Body, using eir considerable mass to catch fast balls, bouncing them high enough for an ally to slam back to opponents. And with eir last teammate chosen, they had three teams, with Keza, Jameela, and emself as captains, and two judges to make calls and run after the balls.

"All right, everyone warm up and get in your plateaus!"

Excitement buzzed through Horace as e hopped into position. It had been ages since e'd last played, early during eir apprenticeship to Clan Zestra, when several members had gathered at a field for a quick evening of sweat and competition. That evening had felt good, like e was a part of the group and could settle with em. It had helped that e was a decent Three Plateaus player—but really, e was decent at a lot of things, just never competent *enough*. Would Clan Zestra have been any different, had e stayed? It was a pointless question to ask. Horace had chosen Aliyah, and even if e never became more than decent at anything, they wouldn't reject em.

Horace turned to their two judges, who each held one of the balls. Keza had brought back several, and e'd picked the two closest to the traditional Three Plateaus size.

"Count to three and throw them up real high. We'll do the rest." E spun to eir team, grinned, and added. "Get ready."

No sooner had e finished that the two crewmates flung the balls high in the sky. The sun briefly blinded Horace as e tried to follow their trajectory, then e spotted one again—and found Keza already leaping for it, claws blessedly retracted as she slapped an open palm into it, aiming in Aliyah's general direction. Aliyah's reflexes kicked in, and they had their foot under it in a flash. It bounced high in the sky, in a weird arc that was sure to land outside the ring. Horace dashed for it, calling Phyllis to get ready—and when e was under it, e used eir thigh to cushion the ball and return it inward with a much more manageable arc. Phyllis swiped at it as it passed, adding speed and a dangerous angle as it flew to Jameela's side.

The second ball was already heading their way, leaving eir team no time to breathe.

The game went on, balls flying and players scrambling, points climbing up and down to cheers and jeers. Horace did eir best to receive the balls coming, using eir experience to redirect it to eir teammates for better attacks. Keza's strategy was the reverse: her team received and set her up for a vicious slam from above. More than once, e raised a cloud of sand as e threw emself to the ground in a desperate attempt to keep eir plateau safe—and more than once, e was rewarded for it by a curse from Keza's side as e successfully salvaged the point. The game lasted a solid, horribly intense ten minutes, with Jameela's team slowly, methodically pulling ahead, using the growing rivalry between Keza and Horace as a distraction to place their shots and score. By the time the judges called the fifteenth and last point, Horace's lungs burned from exertion and eir vision swam. E flopped down on the warm sand.

"That was good." A pause to breathe. The sky above was so pretty, wasn't it? To think e'd once only known it through the pink tint of Trenaze's protective domes, that e'd never collapsed after a frantic Three Plateaus match and stare at its wide blue expanse. "I love life."

"Feels good to move like that again," Keza said. "But you'd better have more than one game in you."

Horace grinned and pushed emself up. "Of course I do! I could play all day!"

And they did. One match after another, rotating the judges to allow new players to join while the rest took a breather. Halfway through the afternoon, Rumi emerged from the Wagon to complain about the noise, and in a matter of minutes he had been roped into the next game as the Hands on Horace's team. Keza made a point of lobbing the ball high over his head, just out of reach, and after a few such maneuvers, Horace unceremoniously grabbed Rumi and threw him up. The artificer panicked and slapped the ball, returning it in an awkward line, but once Horace caught him, he refused to go back down.

"Hold me on your shoulders, big fella! I'm way better like this."

They were allowed an extra player to become the Body, and Horace became an extension of Rumi, running him around as best as e could. Before long, the two other teams also climbed smaller players on shoulders, and the usual rules of Three Plateaus fell apart, giving way to a collective attempt to keep the two balls up in the air as long as they could with an increasing number of piggyback pairs. Aliyah mounted Keza, who somehow managed to both carry them and sometimes intercept a wayward ball with her feet, saving them all.

The afternoon stretched on as the games evolved and changed according to the group's whims, and soon they were discussing the construction of hand nets to catch the other, tinier balls Keza had brought back, and sling them around. The sun vanished as they planned, hidden away by thick grey clouds. A first gust tousled Horace's curls, and as the wind picked up, more and more of the crew stopped talking and turned to the churning seas.

"Storm?" Rumi asked. "The Wagon can take everyone in."

Keza stepped forward, her posture rigid as she scanned the horizon. "Hop on my shoulders, shortscales."

"What—"

She didn't give him time to consider, grabbing him by the neck and hoisting him up. It was not quite as fluid as Horace had seen her do with her kittens and Rumi's flailing made it ten times funnier. E started laughing—until Keza scrambled up eir back, claws out, and the chortle turned into a choked cry of pain.

"Keza!" e protested.

She ignored em, stretching to her full height on eir shoulders, balanced despite the increasing wind.

"You see it, shortscales?"

Rumi did not answer. The ominous weight of his silence lodged itself in Horace's stomach.

"What's wrong?"

"It's glowing," Rumi said. "Gold and cyan, and it's... moving. Slowly, around the island, I think?"

The afternoon cheer vanished, doused by the spreading realization of what Rumi meant. The kraken, the dangerous Fragments that had sunk the *Pegasus*, had tracked them across the ocean. It was here, circling their tiny piece of land.

They were trapped.

6

Those Who Speak

"What now?"

Captain Jameela had herded all four of them into the Wagon, away from the prying ears of her crew. What joy they had scraped together playing Three Plateaus had given way to a low terror, and Jameela clearly thought better of discussing the kraken's arrival in front of them.

Horace felt guilty about it. Shouldn't everyone know? E would have hated to be left behind—and in the past, e had always been part of that crew, the ones who didn't need to hear the details, who'd misunderstand or panic or whatnot. When e had raised a protest, though, Rumi and Keza had loudly agreed with Jameela, and Aliyah had set their fingers on eir wrist.

"I'd feel safer if they did not learn how the kraken tracked us right now, with their emotions so high-strung."

That had felt fairer. Horace would have protected Aliyah, but e didn't want to have to fight the *Pegasus*'s crew, either.

"Don't see how this changes anything for me," Rumi said, answering Jameela's question. "We're not getting anywhere without a good propeller."

"We're not getting anywhere if it crushes your Wagon," Jameela countered.

Rumi thumped the ground with his tail. "It didn't the first time, and it won't this time either."

"You might be willing to stake your life on it, but I'm not."

"Well, tell us when you've got a better idea, Captain," Keza said, leaning forward.

Jameela's gaze slid toward Aliyah, and they chewed on the pipe always present between their black-painted lips.

"I've got nothing. Nothing I'm ready to commit to, anyway. But if you fine people and your legendary happenstances understand any of this mess better, it might be time to put your minds together and try something different. It's *you* this thing is tracking, not us."

"Captain," Aliyah said. "If I have it within my power to stop the kraken from harming us, I will. You have my word."

Jameela huffed, clearly unconvinced, then stomped out to yell at the crew to stop staring out at sea and get building, before the rising winds transformed into a proper storm and they lacked sufficient shelter. Horace turned to eir group.

"What did she mean by 'nothing I'm ready to commit'?"

Tense silence followed eir question, but e knew the others had understood, so e focused on Keza, the most likely of them not to spare eir feelings. She released a soft hiss.

"When you're stalked by something with a specific desire, sometimes the best solution is to offer it to them."

"But that'd mean—oh."

It would mean sacrificing Aliyah to the Fragments. The realization was a rock at the bottom of Horace's stomach, and e turned to them, seeking signs of distress in their knotted brow or pinched lips. They didn't seem happy about the thought, but neither did they share Horace's appalled fear.

"It may be that Rumi is correct, and we can sail past it without ill befalling to the Wagon," Aliyah said. "However, I would rather find what it is that it wants, and if we may help it."

Rumi mouthed "help it" incredulously, and Aliyah's eyebrows shot up.

"Do not discard the idea, Rumi. Your skills were instrumental in repairing the mechanism at Keza's village, and only once we set to the task did the pressure of the Fragments on me relent."

"Yeah, sure, the little Fragments playing with the waterways. That thing sank the *Pegasus*," Rumi pointed out. "I just don't think we should give it what it wants!"

"Might not have a choice," Keza said, "but

that's a moot discussion. If it wanted to chat us up, it could've done that plenty when we were out at sea. Either it can't, or it won't."

Aliyah pressed their lips tight, and cast their gaze out the Wagon's sole window. "If I could touch it while transformed…"

No one had specific suggestions to accomplish that, however, or any alternatives.

With no concrete solution to work toward, Aliyah redoubled their efforts to rebuild the connection with their strange tree transformation powers and the sensitivity to Fragments it brought. Whenever Horace walked into the Wagon, e'd find them sitting crosslegged, eyes either closed or focused on their hands, lost in their own world. E left them to it, uncertain how to help. Across from Aliyah, behind drawn curtains, Rumi continued to tinker, hoping to engineer a speedy propeller.

Outside, the crew argued over who would risk touching the water to check the fishing nets until Keza grabbed a makeshift spear and waded in, unafraid. They'd all seen her fight on the *Pegasus*, and with her proximity to ensure safety, the crew didn't fear the Fragments roaming closer as much. Many had returned to the building of their shelters, a task rendered more arduous by the increasing winds and the hopelessness now weighing their limbs. What was even the point if the kraken never left them?

Horace did eir best to cheer everyone up with hopeful futures. The creature would tire itself and leave them be in time. Rumi would invent a miracle for them, sending them zooming across the waves. Aliyah—their Storm Catcher!—would reach out to it, save them. Somehow they would flee the island. Maybe not today, maybe not in a week, but they would! Except every new day brought the same cloud, the same winds, the same ominous glow circling their island, and the promise that there would be no escape.

One evening, Korrin and Phyllis popped through the Wagon's door, each holding the day's catches wrapped in thick leaves.

"It started drizzling," Korrin said. "Thought

maybe instead of fighting the fire, we could come in and cook on your burner?"

Horace had had eir head in the cupboards, using the opportunity to clean while the supplies were low. Before e could answer, the burner lit with a crackle, its spiral turning orange, and the drawer with the utensils slid open.

"Wagon says yes," Horace chirped.

They both stared, eyes wide, and neither moved to get their fish ready.

"Don't worry, it does that all the time. Moving stuff about is how it communicates with me, since I can't hear it like Rumi and Aliyah."

"It ... didn't do that. At sea, I mean," Phyllis commented, running a hand through her short hair.

Oh. She was right! There had been so many people, and their travel routines had been upended so thoroughly, Horace hadn't noticed how discreet the Wagon had made itself, even after the storm had died down.

"Maybe sailing is hard for it. It had to keep everything tightly shut and all that."

"So it's … sentient?" Korrin asked, finally edging closer to the hot burner.

"Oh, yes, and quite opiniated to boot. One of our first nights together, it helped Rumi and Aliyah cheat at cards, can you believe? As if they needed a hand!"

They laughed at that and, once more at ease, they joined Horace in the tiny kitchen area. E let them handle most of the food preparation, delighting the two with stories of the Wagon's behaviour while the Wagon itself opened cupboards and drawers whenever the two required something. They marvelled every time, and Horace had no doubt the Wagon was enjoying the attention immensely. When they had left, the entire crew's meal prepped, their spirits higher than anybody's had been since the kraken's return, Horace patted the Wagon's stovetop affectionately, dangerously close to its still-hot burner.

"That was fun," e said. "Maybe we should get more crew inside to cook with you in the future."

The curtains to Rumi's workshop snapped

open, and he poked his head out. "They're lucky they caught it on a good day."

All the drawers slammed shut, one of them almost snapping on Horace's fingers, and e laughed, both hands lifted in a peacemaking gesture.

"Now now, don't fight. There's plenty of good days."

Rumi snorted, then blinked several times — the isixi equivalent to humans rubbing their eyes. "Regardless, Aliyah and I need silence to focus. So don't start partying."

"You need rest," Horace countered with a huff.

Rumi had been tinkering late into the night, which e knew from hearing them after Aliyah's new nightmares had woken em up.

They'd begun to dream of entire crews wiped out by a storm, of giant waves crashing on makeshift docks, of terrors that crawled into their skin and startled them awake, clammy and panting, shivering in Horace's steady arms. They talked through the nightmares in the dead of the night, and at times their whispers were accompanied by the worrisome clinks of Rumi's work below.

Aliyah described the nightmares as fuzzy, the words within garbled, the world hazy and changing in rapid, nonsensical ways. Only the water remained—water and people and pain and fear. If not for those, it'd have sounded like almost normal dreams to Horace. Eirs never made much sense to begin with, when e could even recall them.

"Do you believe it?" Aliyah asked one time, their voice a thin whisper in the night.

Horace's half-asleep mind scrambled to shake itself awake. Had e missed a few words, in eir slumbering state?

"Believe what?" e mumbled.

E place eir large hand on Aliyah's bony shoulder, and they leaned into em with a sigh.

"In the Wagon, when we were drifting at sea … you told Jameela it was not my fault."

Horace sat up on their shared mattress, scraping eir shoulder on the wall in eir hurry.

Had they been enduring the blame all this time? That wasn't fair!

"Of course I do! You should, too."

"It tracks *me*, Horace."

"So?" E didn't understand what that changed. "That's what *it* does, not you. You don't control it."

They laughed, then, a sharp and bitter sound e didn't like at all. "You're so sweet."

Something in their tone snagged on Horace's brain, and e needed a moment to recognize it, despite hearing it a hundred times before. Dismissal. That had never come from Aliyah, and it burned a hole in eir stomach, like acid burrowing inside em.

"You think I'm just saying that because I'm your friend. Or that I don't understand."

Horace hadn't expected the quake in eir voice, and it didn't go unnoticed. Aliyah's dark eyes snapped to em.

"Horace, I didn't mean—"

"No, it's all right." It wasn't, not completely. But Aliyah knew e'd stand in their corner no matter what, so they needed someone else to repeat eir words, too. "Come. We're waking Keza up."

E grabbed Aliyah's wrist, pulling them toward the ladder, and within a minute and despite their protest, e was using the broom to poke at Keza, who'd hung a hammock from the rafters and always slept too high for arm's reach. She hissed as she woke, peeking her head out to glare—which, with the moonlight reflecting in her cat eyes, turned out particularly menacing.

"What."

"Do *you* believe Aliyah is to blame for the kraken's attack on the *Pegasus*, or its presence here?"

A low growl rumbled out of Keza. "I don't care what time it is, you tell me who said that and I'll get them sorted."

Horace turned a victorious grin toward Aliyah, and this time their soft chuckles were genuine mirth. "I surrender."

"Wait, *you* thought that?" Keza twisted in her hammock and dropped down, padded feet barely making a sound as they hit the floorboards. The predatory fluidity of her movement had Horace convinced she *would* attack Aliyah, even playfully. "Normally it's Rumi who's got his head up his ass. Look, if you start blaming yourself for all the ways the world goes to shit around you, you'll never end. I thought your thing was to make the best of it, like a deep clean after a bad storm."

"You can't control storms. I control where I go."

"And you'll always be *somewhere*. Don't even start about living as a hermit on a faraway mountain or some shit." Keza crossed her arms, and the judgmental stare she levelled at Aliyah had such a motherly quality to it, Horace melted inside. "Something went wrong. You couldn't transform and save them. It's shit, and it's good that you feel bad over it. But you've got to harness that. Look at Horace: every time e fails, e just trains harder. If your guilt doesn't go into finding a way to prevent stuff from happening again, what's even the point of it?"

Although Aliyah said nothing in response, constraining their reaction to a curt nod, they must have taken Keza's words to heart. They slipped out of bed early the next morning, and spent an hour with their bare feet where the waves would lap at them, eyes closed as dawn spread over the ocean, casting a soft sheen on the distant glow of cyan and gold that marked the kraken's hovering presence. As sailors slowly rose for the day, they would withdraw from the shore and return to the Wagon. The crew's whispers intensified with every new day, but Aliyah ignored them. On the fifth day of practice, Horace would've sworn e glimpsed bark receding into their feet as they left the water. E hurried into the Wagon after Aliyah, and almost bumped into them. They had frozen a step past the entrance, clutching their forehead, as if … in pain?

"Aliyah?"

The name had barely left eir mouth that a wave of intense frustration washed over em. E didn't understand what had provoked that in em—and in truth, it didn't feel like eir own exasperation at all. Aliyah jerked to the side, and turned to stare at a wall.

"Stop it," they growled.

"I'm not doing that!" Horace protested, raising both hands up in innocence. "I swear it's not me."

Another wave hit, and Aliyah's pain morphed into displeasure. "I do not understand what it is you want, but this is painful."

"Can I know what's happening?" Horace asked, not without eir own hint of frustration now. "Because I'm confused."

Surprise arched Aliyah's eyebrows as they turned to face em, as if just realizing e was there. "You feel it, too?" Then at eir nod, "It is this terribly uncouth Wagon we live in. It is very agitated, and intent on making us so, too, or refusing to leave us alone."

All of Aliyah's irritation flew right over eir head, eir own also vanishing as excitement replaced it. The Wagon was talking to em? After all these months with only the opening and closing of cupboards as communication, e was feeling its emotions? Somehow? A wide grin split eir face.

"Hello, Wagon!" e boomed, waving at the air. "Pleased to meet you!"

The Wagon did not answer. Instead, the curtain to Rumi's workshop flew open, and Rumi stepped out, tail twitching behind him. He snapped his teeth in irritation, brandishing a broken piece of wood. "Can't y'all be quiet?"

A low and deep creak of wood interrupted them all. It came from the floor and walls and ceiling, every inch of the Wagon creaking as though caught in strong winds. Yet it had been so silent in the storm, not a peep to be heard as it fought the waves. The sound grew in intensity, snapping and popping at times, until it shaped itself into more than a discordant melody.

"… talk…"

Stunned silence fell over their trio. It had talked—properly talked! The word had been twisted and heavy and scratchy, not unlike Aliyah's voice as they transformed into a tree, but deeper and stranger, a vibration of meaning flitting through the air, so unexpected it might as well have been imaginary. But Horace hadn't dreamed that, not when eir two friends looked equally surprised. So e did the only thing e could think of.

"Yes, talk! I love to talk! I'd tell you to come on in and make yourself at home, but that's not … you're the in and the home."

The creaking rose again, an encompassing orchestra of wooden timbres, from the ceiling and walls and floor, building its way into a single word.

"… negotiate…"

Aliyah gasped, a strangled sound halfway between shock and pain, and knelt on the ground. Horace rushed to their side as they shut their eyes.

"Aliyah?"

"It's—"

A whimper stole their last words. Horace grabbed their hand and squeezed, at a loss about what to do. There was a pressure on eir lung and mind, an insistence to *act* that e didn't understand. Was that the Wagon? The feeling felt vaguer than the previous frustration, harder to pin down.

"Stop it. I told you it's painful!" Rumi was staring at the ceiling, scowling. "This isn't a tinker session. If you have words now, then use them."

Horace didn't understand what was happening, but Aliyah relaxed under eir palm, so that was good, right? Had the Wagon really been hurting them? Why would it do that?

The creaking of wood swelled again, and with it the pressing desire to act returned, stronger than ever. It was all Horace could do not to run out and sprint across the sand and into the sea, and the impulse confused em even more. E forced emself to stay put until the harmony of snapping wood resolved into new words.

"... kraken … sail…"

"I don't understand," Horace said, because usually someone else did, and e wouldn't mind an explanation right about now.

"Honestly," Rumi said, "I'm lost too. Never had *words* from the Wagon before today, or that sort of request."

He made it sound like he had plenty of other requests, and Horace wondered if that's what he'd meant, earlier—if the Wagon could do painful things to Rumi, too. Wouldn't they have noticed if that was the case? The two seemed so close.

They both turned toward Aliyah, hoping for answers. They were staring at their hands, now covered in bark, each finger a long and twisted twig. The transformation! Horace squeezed their shoulder with enthusiasm, but when Aliyah unfurled, only confusion marked their still-elven face. The bark crawled up their neck, and a pale green flickered through their otherwise black eyes.

The Wagon produced a prolonged, splintering wood sound, pushing it until it morphed into " … trust…"

Then it was quiet, not even a small pop to fill the silence.

With a determined resignation, Aliyah replied. "If I must."

They shifted past Horace, tattered cloak trailing as they glided outside, offering no further explanation to Rumi and Horace. Each stride slow and solemn, they walked toward the sea, gaze fixed on the horizon. It reminded Horace of Trenaze's exiles when they took their first steps out of the city's protective domes. Aliyah's slim figure was halfway through the beach, their cloak snapping in the rising wind, their skin half-bark, before Horace understood this was *exactly* like Trenaze's exile. They were going to the sea, and they would not stop within the protection of the shallows.

7

Those Who Hear

Panic squeezed Horace's lungs and e dashed after Aliyah, sand sliding under eir boots as e caught up and placed emself firmly in their path. They stopped without attempting to circumvent em.

"What are you doing?" e asked. "Is there a plan?"

Naturally reserved or not, Aliyah couldn't walk into the kraken's waiting arms—or tentacles, or whichever—without explaining to them why that suddenly seemed a good idea, or what they intended to accomplish. Or why they'd only half-transformed. Or-or anything, really!

"The Wagon believes we can negotiate with the kraken," they said, and there was no scratchiness to their voice, no sign of power reverberating through it. "These shards, the Fragments ... they have history, personality, *goals*. I do not have a good grasp of what the Wagon is trying to explain, but I trust that it experiences the world in a way I do not, and as such carries invaluable wisdom."

"Are you..."

E gestured toward them, unable to phrase any of the dozen questions bouncing around eir mind about their powers. Aliyah's thin lips pressed tighter together.

"I ... believe the Wagon extended itself somehow. To communicate, and to give me this." They lifted the twig fingers before adding, "I trust the Wagon would not lead me astray on a whim, and so I will abide by its request."

Horace turned back to stare at the distant shifting glow, as if the kraken would emerge to reassure em. "So you'll ... walk to it? Talk to it? How does that work?"

"We shall see, Horace."

They brushed past em again, and this time e fell into step with them rather than trying to block the way. Although fear was slowly twisting one knot after another in eir stomach, e knew there'd be no stopping Aliyah from this, not with that fire in their eyes.

"I don't think you should be alone."

A brief smile flitted across their lips. "I am not, am I?"

They reached the water's edge, and Aliyah dropped their cloak then waded in, bare feet digging into the muddy sand. Horace scrambled to remove eir boots and socks and hurry after them, even though e had no idea what use e'd be. It was always better to be there. Before e could catch up, however, Jameela called after em.

"What's going on?"

E spun around, walking backwards through the shallows in order to keep advancing. The captain had rushed to the edge of the water, the remainder of the *Pegasus*' crew forming a wary circle behind her. They'd grown thinner over the last days, their once smiling faces now creased with lines of exhaustion. Everyone was in desperate need of a turn of fortunes.

"We're going to negotiate with the Fragments!"

Jameela's eyebrows shot up, and they tucked their pipe between their lips before crossing their arms. "Don't throw that at me like that's a normal thing to do! Negotiate what?"

Horace shrugged. "No idea, Captain, but it's worth a try."

The water had reached eir waist, so e turned back toward the sea and left Jameela's doubtful stare behind. It took a moment to find Aliyah again; they'd sank all the way to eir shoulders, and their body continued to change, clothes sinking into skin closer to bark, long black braids thickening into dark green lichen. For an instant, e glimpsed roots digging into the sand, holding them steady as they moved forward and plunged fully into the ocean.

That wasn't fair. E couldn't do that, and e had no time to return for Rumi's water-breathing contraption.

"You said you wouldn't go alone," e whispered.

Out in the water, the gold and cyan swirl that marked the Fragments stopped its restless circles. Never had such beautiful colours seemed so ominous to Horace. Eir stomach tightened as the kraken's Fragments brightened, its massive body swimming toward them, terrifyingly fast despite its bulk.

The crashing of waves and howling wind was a symphony of danger, their chaos a reflection of the emotions whirling in em. When e had sworn emself to Aliyah, e hadn't expected it'd be so hard to even *follow* them. What did it matter, how intensely e trained with Keza, when Aliyah strode into stormy waters to face off with a gigantic Fragment? What good was e then?

Soon, Horace could distinguish shards even through the churning waters, each deadly piece covering the power gluing it together—each a threat to Aliyah. The waves crashed into em with renewed vigour, as if to push em away. E held on, swimming closer, treading the water as best as e could. E would not return to the beach without Aliyah.

They'd become visible against the Fragments' light, a thin and craggly tree rooted to the bottom, swaying with the current. Fully transformed, though with nowhere near the number of branches and roots they'd had before. The first time e'd seen Aliyah like this, e'd thought it terrifying, an eldritch being with untold power. Now they seemed fragile, every branch eminently breakable, a sapling of hope e needed to protect.

The bulk of the kraken had to stay in deeper waters, but it extended a long appendage, its movement slow, careful. The tentacle stopped in front of Aliyah, and they reached out in turn.

Aliyah's eyes flared pale green as they touched, the colour melting into the Fragments' golden hues. A surge of growth passed through them, skin thickening, hundreds of twigs expanding from their arms, brown algae clinging to their back, roots digging in the floor. The kraken's tentacle rippled in response, the individual shards floating in a breathing motion, their gold and cyan hues shifting from intense to softer, then back again. Aliyah's own growth seemed to vary in return. Could they truly be talking to them?

Light burst outward before hope could settle in Horace, driving em to shield eir eyes. When e could look again, the tentacle was wrapping itself around Aliyah.

"N-no!"

E pushed against the water, struggling with every step to keep eir balance. E would brute force Aliyah out of there if e needed to, would risk drowning in the attempt, or getting cut into pieces by the Fragments, or being possessed by one of them, doomed to repeat their movements until e died of exhaustion. It didn't matter, e had to try.

The tentacle went two full turns around Aliyah, its shards stretching, letting even more of the light through. They could barely be seen amidst the thick appendage, bits of branches poking through. Except... Horace squinted. The branches weren't poking through, they were *growing* through, unfurling to wrap themselves around the tentacle, looping in and out until the two had become inextricably linked.

Slowly, Aliyah rose out of the water. It was impossible to tell if they dragged the kraken's tentacle up, or if it pulled them out. They broke through the wave together, a beacon in the darkening skies, and Horace couldn't help eir immediate outburst.

"Hey—hi! I'm down here!"

Aliyah inclined their head in eir direction, and Horace would have sworn they'd smiled under all that bark. The tentacle holding them relaxed, easing itself down until it was a platform to stand on, barely wrapped around their legs. They stood there, a dozen branches sprouting all over their body, dripping water into the cracks of a gigantic amalgam of Fragments.

A familiar screech of metal, like iron plates scraping together, thundered across the bay, drawing cries of pain from the crew gathered on the shores. It shifted in tone and intensity, the ear-piercing spikes of it edging out as it morphed on and on, until words emerged from the cacophony—and, Horace belatedly realized, from Aliyah's mouth.

"We are one and many, our stories cut short, our endings stolen. Hear us."

The commanding tone sank into Horace, vibrating deep in eir bones, filled with a compelling power that reminded em of Aliyah's own, in this changed form.

"I-I hear you," e said. "Ears all good."

Somewhere on the shore, Rumi's skittering laugh was followed by a sharp exclamation of surprised pain and a hush—Keza stopping him, no doubt. It helped eir nerves, to know eir friends were nearby, that they were unfailingly themselves, even as e was unfailingly emself, blurting out nonsense.

"No-o," it said, the scraping of metal a strange staccato in the elongated syllable. *"**Hear** us."*

The kraken grew agitated, several appendages slinking in the shallows toward Horace. E fought the urge to swim and scramble back, holding emself as still during the onslaught of waves as e could. The tentacle rose out of the water before em, its light almost all cyan, swirling brighter where the Fragments left circular holes. It waited there, its slow dance through the air almost hypnotic.

Horace glanced at Aliyah, but they only stared at em, wordless. There was only one thing e could think of doing, besides swim-running away. E extended a hand, palm out, to touch the sucker-shaped hole in this great tentacle, the way e'd watched Aliyah do so often before.

"It's the Endless Armada! Dive, now!"

Now? They had too much momentum, would crash into the island before they got enough of a downward angle to avoid the jagged cliffs and pass under. Yveth was a good flyer, with years of escaping the Armada to his credit, but even he wasn't that *good.*

Except five large ships loomed behind them, their sleek form dark blots across the sky, ranks closed and weapons armed. As sure a death as a dive. Might as well perish on their terms.

"Shut down the crystals!" *he yelled back.*

Shock met his command. That wasn't diving, that was dropping. But what choice did they have?

"You heard me! Shut them now!"

The crew obeyed, keenly aware that desperate times meant desperate measures. The familiar hum of their magic went out, and for a moment the entire deck was suspended in silence. Then it tipped forward, plunging down toward the endless sea below, nose-diving. Yveth clung to the wheel; other crewmates had grabbed whatever rope or rail they could. They fell, wind whipping at them, screams caught in their throats. Their highest mast clipped the cliff above and shattered with a loud snap. Fuck, that'd cost a lot to repair. They'd cleared the island though, were under it, still falling.

"ON! Firun, turn it back on!"

He pulled on the rudder, desperate for his ship to right itself. When the hum of magic filled the air again, his own breath returned. If they could only tilt up in time…

The sea kept coming, churning waves ever bigger, ready to devour them. Yveth prayed that they hadn't lit the crystals too late, that the slow recovery would be enough, but still the sea came. He could almost hear it over the whistling wind.

Then they were horizontal and—

The ship buckled as they hit the waves, skimmed them. More cracking wood, more repairs, but they flew back up in a splash. The crew cheered as they rose, a large sky island between them and the Endless Armada.

The cheer died as they regained altitude to find themselves faced with the second half of the Armada, sleek black ships blotting the sky.

Yveth squeezed his eyes shut. There would be no return home for him and the crew, no supplies for the resistance, no victory of the underdog. He knew, deep in his bones, that no amount of epic flying could get them out of this one. That was the end of Pilot Yveth's adventures.

A story untold. Power thrown away.

Wood crept up his legs, popping and crackling as it grew. Yveth fought, twisting and turning until it clamped on his hips then wrapped around his torso, holding him fast.

Was that the end of it? After years in chains, separated from each other, they'd brought the entire crew here, thrown them across the roots. The wood encased him, pressing painfully into his knees, trapping his weakened body. A deep pink glow crawled from an endless pool in the middle, up and up the roots and toward them. He'd thought he'd made his peace with whatever the Empire had in store for him, but fear churned through him with every inch it travelled closer.

He squirmed, to no avail. The roots kept growing, and the pink light edged closer. He could do nothing — nothing but scream in rage. So he did. He screamed until the wood had expanded over his neck and chin, and slipped through his lips to seal them shut forever.

It tasted nothing like the sea winds of his home.

Horace coughed as salt water poured down eir throat. Panic seized eir muscles, and e thrashed until eir head broke the surface and eir feet found the sea floor. E was in the shallows, the tentacle hovering near em, Aliyah still gripped onto it. Had e fallen? Been pushed by a wave? Tried to drown emself? Pain lanced through eir skull as e attempted to figure out what had happened, and as the disorientation slowly settled, a singled word managed to form in eir sludged mind.

"Wow," e said to no one in particular.

A screech of metal answered, worsening eir headache, and Aliyah spoke with the tinny echoes of the Fragments. *"You heard."*

"That's a whole lot more than hearing," e said, "but I did! Or I think I did."

"Free us."

"Oh, that's not me! That'd be Aliyah. They're more than a mouthpiece, you know."

The Fragments slid up, emerging from the water, a hundred different shards spinning together. Agitated, Horace thought. Maybe e shouldn't have been talking to it so casually?

Aliyah crouched down, their body creaking. When they spoke, it was with their own scratchy voice, old wood in the wind rather than screeching metal, and relief passed through Horace.

"It is time for *you* to hear *me*," they said. "We require transportation to the western shores. Tow the Wagon, and I will free you."

Silence.

Even the winds died down, leaving old waves crashing as all gathered on the beach waited, hope held tight in their breaths, for an answer. The tentacle by Horace froze, its slow dance immobilized, the swirl of cyan flecked with gold almost completely still. Horace counted each second as it passed—one … two … three … on and on until e thought eir heart would explode from tension.

The creature retracted, all its tentacles plunging into the water with a splash, so fast Horace barely registered it. Aliyah's surprised cry as they were dragged under pierced eir confusion, and e dove after the tentacle. E reached out toward the glow — as if e could stop this, stop anything — and eir fingers brushed against a shard. It cut, a sharp sting, and the world vanished again.

Hooves beat against the slippery planks as she ran toward the bow. Rain in her eyes, wind whipping at her mane. Once, her wide vision had let her encompass her whole ship, and the sight of it cresting the waves, majestic sails up, had filled her with pride. No need for propellers and sky crystals, not for her, not when the high sea beckoned to her. But the rain had come and never stopped, the storms had worsened with every day, the lightning had struck, again and again, over the course of her voyage. She could see so much of her ship, even now, but it was all destruction, broken masts and snapped rigging, torn sail and missing crew. The water rose, ever closer. The storms had worn them down, little by little, and now the high sea beckoned to her one final time.

To me. Come to me.

A school of fish swims peacefully, silver streaks in the water. We envy them, the simplicity of their story, the beauty of it. They move as one, even if they are multitude. It is a lesson we learn quickly, too, all of us kin, in a way, all of us fragments of what we were, pieces drifting in the water. Our story is not simple, it is not told. We long for the end and the release it promises.

Horace came to in muddled water as hands dragged em to the surface, their claws pricking eir skin.

"Gotcha," Keza said, holding em against a strong current.

Horace muttered some thanks, shaking eir entire body like a big dog to get rid of the daze. When eir blurry vision cleared, eir stomach dropped.

Aliyah stood at the bottom of the sea, out in the depths, roots digging into the mud. Not a single bead of water touched them; it spun around, a terrifying circular whirlpool rising in a conical shape. The kraken swam in it, its massive body pulling the current along, casting gold and cyan hues through the water.

"I tried to reach them, but I can't swim through that, and I couldn't break it up with the staff." With the fur sticking to her bony head, her scowl looked fiercer than ever. "Could barely get you out."

"We have to help," e said.

The tip of Aliyah's branches stretched out, dipping into the whirlpool's spiralling water. Light flashed whenever the kraken sped past them, a mix of pale green and bright cyan or gold. Above their heads, the clouds gathered, swirling in a menacing circle.

"I don't think we can," Keza said. When Horace spun on her, her ears flattened. "I'd love to, friend, but if that thing wanted you there, you'd be there. Drowning yourself won't make

Aliyah safer. Wait and see, and get ready to plunge back in—preferably somewhere drier."

Horace hated the thought, but the weight of eir muscles told em Keza had a point. E'd been fighting the current or threading water since this had started, and exhaustion would soon add itself to the list of threats. Eir fingers throbbed where they'd been cut by the Fragments, blood spilling in the salted water. Still... E couldn't tear eir gaze from Aliyah, drawn to them as surely as if e'd been in the whirlpool's current.

"What are they doing?"

"Negotiating, I think. Feels like there's a back and forth. See?"

As Keza spoke, the kraken surged out of the water to wrap a tentacle around Aliyah. A branch plunged for it, trapping it, and it retracted in a flash of light and a screech of metal. Then Aliyah tore a long root from the mud, wood popping as it crawled closer to the water. A peace offering, Horace thought, and it convinced em to get to safety and let Aliyah handle this. Slowly, e waded toward the shore, Keza in tow.

They joined Rumi and the *Pegasus*'s crew gathered in a silent line and they waited, dripping salt water on the sandy beach. The clouds darkened further, the wind howled, the water roared, and through it all the discordant metal scraping echoed across the shore, winding up Horace ever tighter. Every time it rose, e took an unwitting step forward, until e found emself with water up to eir shins, the occasional wave hitting eir knees.

E was thinking very loudly about the limits of eir patience when the whirlpool crashed on itself.

A dismayed cry escaped em, but before e'd taken more than a stride, Aliyah emerged from the water, standing proudly atop a tentacle. Every branch had fallen from their body, and as the appendage approached the shore, their bark receded into skin. Algae hair transformed back, and when they reopened their eyes, the pale glow was gone. Fully elven again.

"We have come to an agreement," Aliyah declared, and it was their normal voice, thin and deadpan, its true emotion hidden from those who didn't know them well. Horace heard the cautious hope, and eir chest swelled with eir own in response. "We may harness the Wagon to the kraken, and it will tow us to the ocean's western shores."

A mix of alarmed cries and hesitant cheers rose from the crew. Rumi huffed, his tail sending sand flying in a discontent flick, but Aliyah continued before he could raise a formal protest.

"In exchange," they said, and their sudden weariness sent Horace's stomach plunging, "the kraken has demanded that we hear its stories. I will serve as conduit. Is that agreeable to you, Captain?"

They directed the question at Jameela, who turned to scan their crew. Most had grown pale, but Millicent and Korrin offered determined nods.

"Best deal we're gonna get, I think," Jameela agreed.

A wave of light passed through the tentacle in response, and it lowered Aliyah next to Horace. They jumped down, landing by eir side with a small splash, and touched eir forearm. Their voice fell into a whisper. "I might not be myself for the duration of our voyage. Please keep me safe."

"Of course!"

There was so much more e wanted to say — that e'd wished e could have swum in the whirlpool to rescue them, that e wouldn't sleep a wink for months if they needed em to, that no matter where Aliyah's tale led, e would be there, by their side, a shield against the world. But Horace's words, as plenty as they often were, always seemed to fail em when it mattered most. So e picked one to encompass them all, putting all eir love in it.

"Always."

Aliyah smiled, then, and Horace's world felt right again.

8

The Ocean's Tale

They reconvened in the Wagon while Jameela conferred with her crew, and Aliyah crumpled into a chair to rest. Horace brought Keza up to speed regarding what had happened earlier, inside the Wagon. When e mentioned the Wagon's first words and its painful push onto Aliyah, her ears flattened.

"It's an actual, separate person from Rumi?" she hissed.

Rumi snorted. "Of course it is! We told you that the first day you stepped inside, didn't we?"

She sniffed the air, her tail sweeping in an indignant twitch. "I thought you were messing with me. It's *your* Wagon. Why should I expect it to be anything but grumpy like its owner, and eager to annoy me?"

That made Rumi cackle. "If the common denominator isn't me, but you, what does that mean, you think?"

Keza made a half-hearted swipe at him, which he ducked. Aliyah was listening to their bickering with their eyes closed and a hint of a smile, so Horace let it be, enjoying the back and forth until Keza asked.

"So why is it quiet now? Not an opiniated arse like its owner? We've been talking in it and about it like it's not even listening."

It was a good question. It hadn't creaked its way to words, sent waves of feelings, or even slammed a drawer or two to express disapproval since their return. Horace hoped it hadn't reverted to anything but the most basic communication with em. E'd wanted to have long conversations!

"I am *not* an arse," Rumi protested, ignoring the concern about the Wagon itself. "You're just exasperating."

"It is spent," Aliyah cut in. "I believe it was no easy feat to enable my transformation once more, nor is it simple to utter words in our language. However it did that, it may need a long rest to recover."

"Y-yeah, it's gotta be hard," Rumi mumbled. "That's probably why it never spoke to me like that before."

Needling jealousy drenched Rumi's tone, causing everyone gathered to turn to him at once. Horace would have sworn e'd heard something else underneath, a hint of fear e didn't understand. But he'd always been protective of the Wagon, so maybe that was it? E *had* found Rumi splayed out on the floor, whispering to it lovingly, the day they'd landed on the island.

"You're very close to the Wagon," e said. "Are you okay? Do you want to talk about it?"

Rumi slid a step back, hanging by the workshop's curtain, as if to hide behind it. "Close, yes, you could say that. But I'm fine, really! Everything's totally fine. It just surprised me, but it surprised all of us, so what more is there to say?"

He punctuated the question with an awkward, skittering laugh. Between that and his high, agitated pitch, Horace had a hard time believing him.

"You always have more to say. I'm like that too, so I know!" Horace crouched nearby and placed eir large hand on Rumi's tiny shoulder. "When you feel like saying it, come find me."

Rumi laughed again, but instead of dismissing Horace, he patted eir arm. "Maybe I will, big fella. But not now. We have to harness the Wagon to a giant cephalopod of Fragments, *somehow*, so I've got my work cut out for me."

He threw his best glare at Aliyah, and everyone understood the remark as the plea for a return to normal it was. Aliyah inclined their head.

"You will forgive me for adding to your endless workload, I hope."

"We'll see about that once we reach continental shores."

And with that, he scampered outside, away from their collective gaze and silent questions.

The moment he was out of the door, Keza let out a low rumble.

"What d'you think is wrong with him?"

"I don't think anything is *wrong* with him," Horace said. "He's been with this Wagon forever, or close enough, no? You've seen him with it. Of course he's upset that it talked to Aliyah first, and not him. Or maybe he's just upset that things are changing a lot."

"Hmrph. I bet there's a secret," Keza said—and of course she'd think that when she kept so many herself, concealing her life from before the Wagon to any but Horace, who'd witnessed it. "But as long you think he's all right."

Quiet warmth filled Horace. She was *worried*. For all the sharp words Keza and Rumi traded, they never missed a chance to care about one another. E grinned.

"I do. Besides, if he keeps a secret the same way he keeps his game strategies to himself, we'll know all about it very soon."

The crew dedicated the next day to stocking up on provisions, either fishing or foraging the island for edible fruits. No one knew how long it would take them to reach the western continent, and a full cold box seemed the least of precautions.

While most others gathered food, Rumi and Horace had worked together—Rumi directing and Horace diving—to tie the Wagon to the Fragments with vines or regular ropes. The creature had rearranged itself, several minuscule Fragments forming hoops along its main body, the middle a shardless ooze of glowing light through which e could secure the rope. Horace used the breather Rumi had crafted for em in Alleaze, every underwater movement carefully calculated to avoid cutting emself on a Fragment. It was eerie, to float amongst the metallic shards, their gold and cyan glow brushing against eir skin as they hovered in the water, slow and peaceful. E might have thought the amalgam docile, if not for the striking memory of its attack on the *Pegasus*.

It took a dozen ropes and vines passed through the kraken then attached to a system of pulleys and anchors Rumi had built for the Wagon to be securely tied while maintaining the flexibility required to ride the inevitable waves or withstand the potential slight dives of the kraken. No one mentioned the creature could sink them on a whim, should it change its mind. Aliyah trusted it not to, and that was enough for Horace. It seemed to be enough for the crew, too, though most prayed for the Sea Spirit's protection as they climbed aboard the Wagon, now bobbing in the depths on its floater, above the kraken.

Captain Jameela was the last one to come aboard, and as most of the crew settled inside, they scaled the ladder to the Wagon's roof, where Aliyah was sitting, cross-legged and eyes closed, a thin stripe of bark running up their neck. As asked, Horace guarded them, though e didn't know against what. Meanwhile, Rumi gave his mechanisms one last thorough verification.

"Still certain about this, Storm Catcher?" Jameela asked.

"Certainty is a luxury none of us can afford," they said, "but I believe this is our best chance. May it become a story we survive to retell until it passes into legends."

A sharp laugh escaped Jameela, and she stuck her pipe, unlit between her teeth. "I can get behind that. Let's sail, then."

Rumi grabbed a crank and spun it, shortening the vine cables below and pulling them out of the shallows, toward the kraken. After watching him struggle for two turns, jumping up and down to use his weight to help, Horace offered to take over. Rumi let em, panting, and instead surveyed the waters and the lengths, to signal Horace when to stop. Once he was satisfied, he nodded to Horace.

"All ready to go. You might wanna hold Aliyah when they give the signal."

Horace thanked the glyphs for that advice, because Rumi had barely scampered downstairs when Aliyah must have wordlessly asked the kraken to swim—and it was *fast*. In the space of a blink, they went from floating by the island's shores to speeding across the open sea with no land in sight. Every wave sent them soaring through the air and crashing back down, sea water splashing part of the platform, and had Horace not held Aliyah and the railing, they might have fallen overboard from the initial surprise.

They had barely sailed for a few minutes when Aliyah's skin cracked and transformed.

"It is time for me to uphold my end of the bargain," they said. "It would be best, I think, if I remained inside."

Many crewmates read their return downstairs as a signal that they could leave the cramped Wagon, and they climbed the ladder to enjoy the wild ride, eager to sink into the exhilarating bumps rather than to think of the terrifying creature dragging them along faster than they'd ever sailed. Keza either clung to the highest point of their makeshift mast—now without sail—or hid underneath to avoid the water.

Horace loved the spray above, but e almost never abandoned Aliyah's side. They sat on their shared bed, branches sprouting through the tattered cloak to grip the Wagon's wall behind. Their eyes remained open, their light sometimes golden, sometimes cyan, but never the pale green that Horace had grown used to. Words flowed ceaselessly out of their lips, the voice soft, scratchy, and compelling.

They told the story of a munonoxi sea captain caught in interminable rain and storm, who drowned with her ship without ever seeing the sun again.

They told the story of a shoemaker barely making ends meet, whose shop served as a front to a group of mismatched, down-on-their-luck residents who spoke of revolution, galvanized by recent plans to relocate their entire neighbourhood.

They told the story of an insomniac human elder who filled countless nights with the *tap-tap-tap* of her needles until death came, a sudden chest pain pulling at her core.

They told the story of a felnexi with their ears clipped, who skulked about in the dark of night and eavesdropped on terrible state secrets, only to find magic had frozen each of their limbs, trapping them, a fly in a web.

They told the story of so many sailors, some on the waves, others on the wind; so many early deaths, so many sudden ones.

On and on they went, until their throat was parched and they broke from the hold. Horace sat and listened, absorbing the tales of countless strangers, water at the ready for Aliyah whenever they emerged from the trance. They never did for long, sipping briefly before sinking into the next story. Neither of them slept the first night, but when the sun rose, then passed its highest point, Horace intervened. E placed a hand on Aliyah's shoulder and used the short drinking time to plead.

"You need longer pauses. Please, tell it you have a body to sustain."

Lines of exhaustion creased their face where the bark had not yet grown, though it seemed to spread with every tale. "There are so many, Horace."

"So endurance is crucial," e insisted. "A meal every day, at least, and some sleep if you can."

Aliyah slumped against the wall, but nodded in agreement. "I did tell you to keep me safe."

They eventually fell into a cycle, with Aliyah holding off the kraken long enough to eat every day. Sleep continued to escape them, however: every time they lay down to rest, the stories would return, slipping in their dreams and forcing them back awake—or whatever one should call their trance-like state as they spoke the tales aloud.

They never did collapse, however. They shared hundreds of tales over the course of the voyage, more names and details than Horace could ever hope to remember. Some lasted but a few minutes, while others spawned a lifetime and several hours of telling; some captured a single moment with perfect clarity, others bounced around a chaotic life with no narrative thread to help parse the story.

Every new story—every new *Fragment*—sank into Horace, cutting something deep and invisible. Who were these people? Most didn't name places e knew of, sometimes describing impossible things such as flying islands and ships, or feats of magic e'd never seen any rune trigger. Were they all imaginary, tales unfinished and abandoned? It was so hard—so terrible—to think of them as real people, as Aliyah believed. The questions haunted em as surely as Fragments haunted the lands and seas, roaming in eir mind whenever a rare silence filled the Wagon, nagging at em.

As time passed, Horace would have sworn the kraken dwindled under them, from a colossal amalgam of Fragments to a big, clearly octopus-shaped creature. It had grown on em during eir visits up top, the sight no longer terrifying but almost beautiful, a tranquil glow that marked their passage through the sea, its long tentacles trailing behind the Wagon.

Still ... when Keza—perched once again on the mast—called for everyone to come see the land on the horizon, Horace was relieved for their sailing to come to an end.

This time, the first thing to snag Horace's attention was not the broken ocean, as e'd called it, but the broken sky. Thin dark lines rose through it, columns of smoke from multiple fires. An excited wave passed through the crew at the obvious signs of civilization, and a hearty speculation began about which city this might be. Millicent, the best navigator amongst them, oversaw the debate with a smirk, withholding her answer.

Aliyah emerged onto the Wagon's top platform, their every step weak and hesitant. No bark remained on their skin, but the dozen days narrating endless stories had taken their toll. They gripped the railing and wordlessly leaned against Horace, so e did what e did best, and babbled about the cool sharp cliffs coming into view, the flocks of birds taking off from them and scattering about, the excitement of a new leg in their journey, on a whole new continent!

The kraken guided them into a rocky nook,

and with land so close, it was striking how much smaller it had gotten. It occupied most of the alcove still, but it would never have fit upon departure from the island. When Horace commented on how much harder it'd make untangling themselves, Aliyah set a hand on eir arm.

"No need."

Their voice became scratchy with the two words, legs turning into long roots that wrapped themselves all around the Wagon's railing and wonky outside pipes. They lowered their body, holding on to the Wagon through branches, and the kraken lifted a tentacle out of the water to meet them. Aliyah extended a hand of bark and twigs and flattened it against one of the glowing suckers. They were beautiful, together, eerie colours in the cliff's shadows.

"Your story is my story," Aliyah intoned, the cadence and words now so familiar that Horace whispered them along eir friend. "Your pain is my pain. Your joy is my joy. Your life is my life."

The Fragments stopped their endless spin,

hovering in their gold and cyan shine, caught in the swirl of Aliyah's power. It rippled out of them, fully returned, a pressure on the world, a command for attention, for dedication.

"Your stories are my stories," they finished, softer than they'd ever had.

The kraken's glow shifted into a bright light under Aliyah's palm, then the shards around dissipated, the effect rippling outward, the entire creature turning into sparkling powder before sinking into Aliyah's arms, fusing into it. The bark evaporated alongside the Fragments' dust, and Horace suddenly remembered what it'd mean for Aliyah. E scrambled over the railing, heart bouncing in panic, and held to it one-handed as e stretched out and wrapped an arm around Aliyah's waist. E caught them just as the roots retracted, vanishing with the last inch of the kraken.

They slumped into eir arm, frail and unconscious once more.

Conversations erupted amongst the *Pegasus* crew, awe and wonder undermined by a single, obvious question: why hadn't Aliyah saved them the first night, while their ship still stood? Keza helped Horace back onto the platform, and e held Aliyah protectively against eir chest. When Jameela turned to them, the crew hushed, clearly awaiting an explanation.

"They tried," Horace said, hoping it'd be good enough. "They tried, and the most they could do was save Korrin. We don't understand it either."

Horace pushed through the crowd, eager to climb down the ladder and escape the crew's scrutiny. Behind em, e heard Keza suggest they raise sail and head toward the smoke lines, and Jameela took it as a signal to get her crew to work.

With the excitement from their arrival dwindling, eir own exhaustion began to sink in. Horace settled Aliyah into their bed, then leaned against the nearby wall. E'd only slept in short fits, forced away from Aliyah by Keza when she'd realized e had no intention of resting unless someone took eir place. Horace had wanted to listen in, to absorb the stories shared and remember as much of them as e could. It had been important to the kraken, like all these Fragments had coalesced with that single goal. Had the Wagon known?

It hadn't said anything since those first words, but the cupboards had held tight, and not a drop of water had made it through its walls, no matter how hard the waves crashed against it as they sped across the ocean. Horace hoped it'd get talkative again once they landed. E patted the floorboards under em.

"I want to have conversations, even if you do turn out to be opiniated and grumpy."

Horace could have sworn e felt a hint of warmth, but e was so tired, e might have wished it into existence.

An hour and a solid nap later, Horace sought the only member of their team with any sense of how big the world really was.

Rumi sat in his workshop, his latest propeller attempt discarded. He wasn't tinkering, not even sketching some rough ideas, and not whittling at a piece of wood, which was his usual activity to brainstorm or push boredom away. He sat on his stool, his claws tapping a slow rhythm on the workbench, his gaze lost somewhere distant.

He'd stayed hidden here for most of the trip, rarely dropping by Aliyah's endless string of stories and skipping meals with worrisome frequency. Horace hadn't had time to truly check on him, but Keza said he had promised to eat then told her off, which felt "normal enough". The last Horace had seen him, he'd peeked upstairs to watch the land approach, then muttered at the smoke lines, clacked his teeth, and scampered right back to his workshop. It hadn't occurred to Horace he'd meant to hide again, and now that e'd recouped, e refused to let it slide any longer.

"Rumi."

Rumi jumped, startled by eir voice, then spun on eir stool toward Horace. "Oh hey! Didn't hear you. Everything good up there?"

"Maybe? I was napping." Horace pulled the curtain close behind em. "They meant to use the sail to get near those smoke lines. I thought we could look at the big map again, and you could tell me where we're heading?"

Rumi huffed. "I don't need the map to tell you that's Virze. Way farther south than I wanted to be."

There had been a hitch in Rumi's voice when he'd named the place, and now his friend was looking anywhere but at em. This wasn't a simple geography matter.

"You know it well?"

A strained, skittering laugh escaped him. "Sure do. That's the city I was born in, but I don't think I'm more welcome there than Keza is in hers. It's bigger, though, so we can get supplies and be on our way before trouble comes calling."

Horace didn't like the sound of that. There had always been a bittersweet quality to stories Rumi told of his home—great festivals of creations, beauty in every corner, and a love for puzzles and challenges that Horace saw reflected in many of Rumi's wooden toys—but he'd seemed like he admired and missed it. If e'd had to guess, Horace would have thought he visited regularly, just not as often as the road permitted. He'd never mentioned any sort of exile.

"Are you sure? If someone's a problem, we'll be there for you."

Keza would give them all a good trouncing. Only *she* got to make fun of Rumi.

"I'm sure, Horace." He slid down the stool, his tail thumping on the ground like the period at the end of his choice. "Besides, the Wagon can't get in. It'll have to wait for us outside, and after those new words? I'm not keen on parting with it for long."

And with that, he slipped out of the workshop, leaving Horace with no chance to reply. Maybe that was best. Horace didn't know whether e wanted to plead for time to discover Virze, prod Rumi to understand why he was so intent on avoiding it, or explode with eir own excitement at the Wagon's first and future words.

There would be time for all of those—and so much more—but eir stomach grumbled, a firm reminder of more immediate matters. They had made it across the ocean, and although it had cost them dearly, Horace thought they all deserved a feast in remembrance and celebration of all the lives lost at sea, from the countless stories shared by Aliyah to the sailors who'd been taken with the *Pegasus*.

As it turned out, e got eir wish the following morning. Once the Wagon had climbed back ashore within walking distance of Virze, everyone had agreed to settle for the night. Rumi and the crew had built a makeshift smoker for the freshly caught salmon, and the fish cooked overnight while Horace set dough to rise with the last of their flour stock. Keza rose early to scavenge and returned with a wide variety of berries and a few apples, one of which Horace unceremoniously grabbed for emself. Stories from eir youth made these out to be so common, but e'd rarely seen any in the desert.

The apple turned out delicious and fresh, and

Horace had to hold emself back not to snatch a second one—there hadn't been enough for all of them, let alone for em to take two. Jameela's crew spent a good part of the meal grilling Horace about their previous encounters with Fragments, and after a glance to confirm Aliyah didn't mind em sharing, e recounted the strange attack in Trenaze that had led to eir meeting with Aliyah, using a bun of bread as replacement for the Fragment Amalgam as e reenacted its swooping into the shield domes. The delighted sailors met the tale with plenty of gasps and exclamations, but when they pushed for more, Jameela cleared her throat and reminded them they needed to plan their time in Virze, turning the conversation to more practical matters.

Captain Jameela and two of the more experienced sailors knew the local language, so they decided to get hired as dockworkers and deckhands, either together or in small groups, until they could join a crew from Virze that was heading across the ocean, back to Alleaze. Rumi offered them most of the gadgets and toys he had built to sell, to help them fund their stay for a while.

"Won't *we* need that?" Keza asked.

"I can create more before we follow."

After what he'd mentioned the previous day, Horace desperately wanted to ask more about Virze and why he thought he wouldn't be welcome there. But if Rumi hadn't said anything then, Horace doubted he'd share more in front of Jameela's crew, so e shoved a bit of bread in eir mouth to keep the question there. There would be time: they had chosen to give the Wagon a few days to recover and plan their own time in Virze.

All too quickly, the breakfast was gone and the crew had helped clean out the plates and gathered what little belongings they had. Horace's heart squeezed when they congregated near the coastline trail that headed toward the smoke lines and the city, still half a day away.

"Well," Jameela started, with the tone of someone about to say their goodbyes, and that alone was too much.

Horace sprinted forward, to wrap them in a

big hug and lift them up, triggering a smattering of chuckles from the crew. E moved to the next in line, holding Millicent so tight she complained about her old bones, then gave Korrin the same treatment. The young sailor thanked em for the ship rescue, then advised that Horace keep practising eir bluffs for kerva. By the time e had given all the sailors their hugs, hot tears streamed along eir round cheeks.

"Good luck," e said, eir words choked with emotions. "We'll always remember the *Pegasus*."

Behind em, Rumi mumbled, "Not all of us for the same reasons."

The immediate laughter his comment triggered lifted some of Horace's sadness, and e dropped a hand over Rumi's shoulders to pat it.

"Safe travels, if you can have them," Jameela declared, "and may you find your answers."

Then she gestured at the crew to turn around, and the sailors waved their final goodbyes before heading on the road. The four of them watched them walk away until the coastal trail dipped out of view.

They were only gone a few seconds before Horace couldn't hold eir silence any longer. E turned to the others, eir smile still wavering from the earlier tears.

"How long before the Wagon talks again, you think?"

Aliyah smiled at em, but it was Rumi who replied with an annoyed flick of his tail.

"If I know anything about it, we should take bets on whether it'll ever shut up once it begins."

"Oh, lovely. As if you lot weren't noisy enough," Keza commented.

Rumi huffed. "I'd rather hear it than you!"

Then they were off again, bickering as if nothing had changed and they were still on the other side of the ocean. Horace glanced back at the endless shimmering water, eir mind lingering on the countless stories the kraken had shared through Aliyah. E wondered how many more Fragments were out there, swimming deep beneath the waves, desperate for someone to listen to their tales.

"They're everywhere," Aliyah said, as though

they could hear eir thoughts. "We have to go forward."

"To the grove," e said, "you're right."

There would be plenty more Fragments on the road ahead.

THE STORY CONTINUES....

Fate and friendship brought Horace, Rumi, Keza, and Aliyah together in Rumi's sentient self-propelling wagon. They seek the forest haunting Aliyah's dream, hoping for answers about the elf's past and unique abilities—but first, they need to traverse a world haunted by Fragments, dangerous shards that can possess travellers and react to Aliyah's presence.

They've reached Virze, a marvel of art and engineering and a city in which all acts of creation are beloved, but Rumi desperately wants to avoid his hometown and the demons of his past.

When the Wagon crew realises half of those might be fears of his own making, however, they refuse to leave. But between the curse that ran him out of town and the source of his engineering skills, Rumi has been keeping even more secrets than they'd expected. He'll need all their support to face the loved ones left behind and prove to all, himself first and foremost, what he is truly capable of.

Excerpt from *MOTES OF INSPIRATION*

With every new year of failures, every new incident that left either him, his work areas and tools, or his current mentor more damaged than before, the rumours had swelled.

Cursed to stagnate. Cursed to destroy. A danger to everyone around.

Rumi didn't want it to be true. It couldn't be. He had so many ideas all the time, and he tried so hard to make them work. Everyone looked at his plans and said it should work. That's what he repeated the small voice in his head that told him to give up, to stop pretending he could achieve anything. It grew louder every day, but Rumi pushed on. Sooner or later, he'd succeed. He'd take the plan and build a prototype out of it, and no one would be wounded. No accidents. He was not a force of destruction.

That sooner or later had to be today, at Elzear's Showcase of Shining Minds. The Festival was meant to give room to the creativity of Virze's younger generations with all manners of Shaping. It encouraged trying out new ones, combining skills, bringing results that were unexpected, good or not. All in honour of the great Elzear, who had been said to dabble in countless crafts and skills, and who had travelled the world to share with everyone the ways he could shape the world. He didn't even need to be perfect. He just needed not to blow anything up.

"I'm ready, Pops."

Order the next book now at
books2read.com/motesofinspiration-nerezia

JOIN THE NEWSLETTER TO GET ALL EXTRAS AND
NEVER MISS AN UPDATE

About the Author

Claudie Arseneault is an easily-enthused aromantic and asexual writer with a never-ending cycle of obsessions but an enduring love for all things cephalopod and fantasy (together or not!). She writes stories that centre platonic relationships and loves large casts and single-city settings, the most notable of which are the City of Spires series (2017-2023) and Baker Thief (2018).

In addition to her own fiction, Claudie has co-edited Common Bonds (2021), an anthology of aromantic speculative short stories. She is a founding member of The Kraken Collective, an alliance of self-publishing SFF authors, and the creator of the Aromantic and Asexual Characters Database.

Find out more at claudiearseneault.com

Start another book from the Kraken Collective!

Craving more fun bite-sized queer fantasy? Party of Fools is a comedic adventure with big Final Fantasy vibes where two rebels tag along as the Chosen One and imperial Hero escapes scrutiny to go on a worldwide food tour—that is, if she can escape the Capital.

Dig into another novella lead by a non-binary protagonist and thaes close-knit group of friends with *The Shimmering Prayer of Sûkiurâq*, A deliciously queer magical person story in a secondary world with floating cities and airships, perfect for fans of She-Ra and Steven Universe.

**Find these books and more at
www.krakencollectivebooks.com**

Acknowledgements

Stories from the Deep marks a special moment from me: after years (more than a decade!) of almost accidental (at first) cephalopod internet branding, I finally have a story with a kraken. And of course it's both majestic, beautiful, dangerous, and containing multitudes. Maybe, just maybe, the kraken is a metaphor.

Normally, I don't know with whom to start acknowledgements. This time, though, the shiny spot goes to my cover artist, Eva I., who continues to bring this series to life in one long canvas, and who has created an incredible piece of art with this cover. It is all I could have dreamed of, and I am so incredibly thankful for her care, patience, and clever problem solving in every little detail of it.

This series would not exist in its current form with the insightful feedback of Quartzen, Cedar, and Lynn, and it wouldn't be anywhere near as cleanly written without Lynn's thorough editing.

But writing such a long series of novellas is a

journey of its own, and it wouldn't happen without my numerous support system: family and friends encouraging me to write, my friend ravenously grabbing every novella proof copy the moment I get them (you know who you are), my partner steadfastly supporting the wild mood swings that come with the writing life, my online communities and readers clamouring for more queer books with no romance. Everyone who loves this crew, memes on them, reviews their story, recommend them to others, or even draws fan art..! You continue to make *their* story *your* story, too.

So thank you all so much. Your love keeps me going—onward to the fifth novella!

www.ingramcontent.com/pod-product-compliance
Ingram Content Group UK Ltd.
Pitfield, Milton Keynes, MK11 3LW, UK
UKHW020907020125
453198UK00006B/10

9 781738 925964